DALTON'S KISS BOOK 3

KATHI S. BARTON

This is a work of fiction. Names, characters, places, and incidents are products of the author's imagination or are used fictitiously and are not to be construed as real. Any resemblance to actual events, locations, organizations, or persons, living or dead, is entirely coincidental.

World Castle Publishing, LLC
Pensacola, Florida
Copyright © Kathi S. Barton 2021
Paperback ISBN: 9781955086059
eBook ISBN: 9781955086066
First Edition World Castle Publishing, LLC, April 26, 2021
http://www.worldcastlepublishing.com
Licensing Notes
Cover: Karen Fuller
Editor: Maxine Bringenberg

Prologue

CJ stretched out on the lawn chair and looked up at the sky. It would be snowing before morning, and she, for one, was looking forward to the cold that would end things for a while — bugs and the like. Smiling, she stood up and felt the snap of the cold touch her skin. The way the breeze blew through her hair, making it feel colder when it touched her skin again. Once she made her way into the house, she gathered up the things to make some brewed tea. She'd not had any in so long her mouth was watering for a little sip.

"I heard you come in. Have you had enough sunshine today?" Circe Jane Montgomery told her sister, Pfeiffer, that she'd never have enough sunshine. "The rest of us in the world are scrambling for something warmer, and you're outside without a coat. Or shoes, for that matter."

"I love the cold." That was an understatement. CJ couldn't think of a word that would say how much she loved the cold. "I was thinking of having a nice cup of apple tea. Would you like a cup?"

"I would love one. Also, I baked apple scones yesterday." She told her sister that was more than likely the reason she'd been craving it. "Could be. Before I forget to tell you yet again, there is a schedule opening at the store in the morning for you if you'd like to pick it up."

"I would love to pick it up." She would love to go to work tomorrow. That would leave her the rest of the day to do her other job. The one that paid their bills and made sure they had money in the bank. Working was one of the many ways she helped her big sister. "Are you and the girls going to be working on cookies tomorrow? I know they are planning the entire day around being with you."

"They've told me. I don't know how much energy I'll have for it, but I'm going to spend the day with them." Pfeiffer wasn't just her big sister, but she was her much older one. There was almost twenty years difference in their ages. Pfeiffer's daughters, Sally and Rachel, were about the same age as CJ. "I saw that you picked up the ingredients for snickerdoodles. Don't you like any other cookie than that?"

"I *can* eat other cookies, but I don't like them as much as I do those. Sally makes them just right, just enough cinnamon to sugar all over them." Both her nieces could cook and bake like their mom. CJ was lucky if she could brew a pot of tea without forgetting about the water until it was all gone. Twice that had happened to her. "When is Rachel coming home?"

"Tonight sometime. She said she was going to drive straight through. I begged her not to, but she's as stubborn as you are." That, she was sure, her sister didn't think of as a compliment. "Then we're all going to get up early and go out for breakfast."

CJ would join them in their baking if she was off, but she didn't enjoy herself. She did love them all, but they were mother and daughters, and having her there made them have to divide their time with her too. She wanted them to spend time with their mother. CJ would if she still had hers around.

Sipping her tea with her sister, they talked about the cookies they were going to bake. The three of them could have several hundred dozen cookies baked in two days and not eat a single one of them. CJ would be sick after eating a lot of cookie dough and then trying any cookie that came out of the oven. Her weakness was sweets. But her biggest was snickerdoodles.

At six, they both sat in the living room to watch the news. Dinner was over, they'd cleaned up the kitchen, and now this was the time they settled into the couch. CJ didn't much care for sitting idle, so she would work on her laptop to get a fresh start for the morning.

The house belonged to her sister now, so she set the rules for the television. Before that, their mother had owned it. Mom had left the house to the two of them. When things got to the point where Pfeiffer needed to take a loan out for college for Sally, Pfeiffer bought her out so she could use the house as collateral. CJ never bothered having it transferred back into her name. It wasn't something she was worried about.

When the news was over, they watched a couple of game shows. It was a nightly thing they both had been doing before their mom passed away. It was also their time to talk about what was going on around town, which Pfeiffer knew the most about.

"Did I tell you that Mr. Rogers got off with no fine and no jail time?" CJ loved that old man and would have taken him to see his wife had she known. "There is a new program getting started to help people out that don't have much in the way of food or transportation. I hope it works out. There are a lot of people out there that need help most of the time."

They had too before she got a good job. Like when a big bill came due at the same time as the taxes. It didn't happen as much as it used to, not with them simply not using the credit cards to pay for things.

Borrowing from a credit card company to pay the electric bill or whatever was coming due had nearly made them lose their home.

They were doing all right now. Sally had graduated from college to be a teacher at the same time CJ had. Rachel was in her last year. As soon as Rachel graduated, she'd get a good job as a nurse and be able to pave her own life.

"I heard from the bank again today." CJ asked her what he had wanted. "Other than for me to go out with him, he wanted to know if we wanted to refinance this house. I have no idea why we'd want to refinance a house that we own. I told him no again and no to the dating thing too. I'm not ready for that."

"Not that I think you should date Daniel Benson, but you really should be dating again." Pfeiffer just looked at her. "Okay, we both should be dating, but it's been almost ten years. Aren't you ready to get your body waxed up for some sex-starved man?"

"He would have to be sex-starved to want to sleep with me." CJ told her sister they didn't usually do much sleeping when they were sex-starved. "Very funny. When are you going to date again? I think it's been longer than I have since you went out on a — Oh, CJ, I'm so sorry."

"It's all right." She looked away so her sister wouldn't see the hurt. "It's been a while, I know that. But he hurt me, and I'm afraid. It took me four years to learn it wasn't my fault, even though he blamed me and to say that he hurt me. I think it was money well spent."

They didn't speak for a few minutes, and she was all right with that. She and her sister could go days without really talking about anything serious, and it never really bothered either of them. Sometimes the quiet was better than emptying out one's brains, as her grannie said.

"I was just thinking of Grannie myself." Pfeiffer was like that. She could latch onto whatever a person was thinking without a second thought. "When was the last time you saw her? I've not been in about a week. She doesn't like me as much as she does you anyway."

"She loves you. And the girls. I went to see her just this morning on my way back from my run. Grannie still asks me why I run if there isn't anyone chasing me. But we had a nice talk. And she and I had breakfast together." Pfeiffer asked her if that was her second or third breakfast this morning. "I do believe it was only my second this time. Anyway, she was telling me about this blanket I should make. I don't know where she comes up with this idea that I can quilt, but she always has a rough draft of a pattern when she thinks of one."

"You look so much like Mom. Maybe that's it. Mom loved to quilt. She wasn't as good as Grannie, but we stay warm all winter with her quilting. Well, most of us do. Do you have any more than a sheet on your bed in the winter months?" CJ told her she had one quilt on her bed. "Small wonder. I remember Dad being like you are, overheated all the time. However, I don't think I ever saw him walking around in the snow without shoes on. It's a miracle you have any feeling in your feet at all."

"I have lots of feelings in my feet, thank you very much." They both laughed, and CJ asked her why she'd brought up Grannie. "I was just thinking about how she would always have some saying about something you were doing. Like emptying your brains out."

"Yes, she did at that. I remember thinking she was nuts when I was a kid. She'd say something like that and then just walk away like I was supposed to be able to decipher whatever the heck she was talking about. My least favorite one was, 'Bachelor's wives and maid's children are well taught.' That is a contradiction all the way around."

"Of course it is. I know the meaning. Do you want me to explain it to you?" Pfeiffer looked at her oddly, and CJ smiled. "I promise you I know what it means. It means that a childless man and a childless woman have no knowledge about maintaining a good idea about things they don't have. You see? They have these opinions about child-rearing that are wrong because they have nothing to base it on."

"Okay, that does make it sound right. What other tidbits of information do you have about her sayings? Let me think of one."

While her sister thought about what Grannie used to say, CJ read over the email that had just entered her box. It was from her boss. As her emails were coded, she put in the password to open it up.

"Something wrong?"

"I'm not sure. I have this email about the last job I did. He's saying he didn't get it. However, not only does it have the work order number on it that I assigned, but the attachment is attached to the reply he sent." Pfeiffer asked her if that made better sense in her head. "Yes. What I mean is, I attached the job to an email that he just replied to me on. On it is the attached job. It's been opened too. The email and the attachment."

"How do you know he opened them?" She said her email told her that. "You can fix it, so you know if someone opens your email? I'd like to have that on mine. I have people telling me all the time they didn't get their bill."

"I'll fix it for you in the morning. Not only will it tell you if someone opened it, but also which computer it was opened on. Like you'd know it was me that opened it because of the IP address that's there." She looked at her sister's expression. "You have no idea what I'm talking about, do you? How can you live here with me and not have a clue what I'm going on about most of the time?"

"Because you're brilliant, and I'm just a homebody that loves you to pieces?" CJ hugged her as she dug into the popcorn bowl. "As for Grannie, I'm not sure I will ever figure her out. She's a great deal like you in all ways. I think I remember her being warm all the time too. Must have skipped me. Thankfully." CJ laughed.

They watched television until ten, then CJ went up to her room. She didn't go to bed but worked from her computer for a while before she'd lay down. Never being one that needed a full eight hours of sleep, CJ could sleep for an hour or two before getting up fresh as a daisy.

Not her sister or nieces. If they didn't get at least eight or nine hours, they were crabby all day. And she'd never get in the way of their first cup of coffee. CJ didn't have vices like that to get her going. She could even skip eating a meal sometimes.

Her phone ringing woke her from a dead sleep. It took her only seconds to realize the person on the other end of the phone had the wrong number. She asked him to slow down and say what he needed once more.

"I've found a woman on the side of the road." Okay, CJ sat up in her bed, pulling on clothing as he continued. "She's been hurt badly, and I'm helping her along. The last number she called was this one. I don't know her name, but I was wondering if you could meet me at the hospital."

"Where are you?" He told her which road he was on and the mile marker. "Okay. You said the woman had been beaten up. Can you tell me what she looks like?"

Instead of answering her, she got a picture of the woman. It was her niece Rachel, and she did look really bad. Her mind skittered over his comment that he was helping her along, and she refused to think he was helping her along by hurting her more. CJ grabbed her keys and was out the door before she spoke again.

"I'm on my way. The hospital closest to you is Mercy. Can you get her there?" He said he was standing outside their emergency room doors now. "What are you? Who are you?"

"My name is Brian. Vampire. Are you going to have a hissy fit now about this?" She asked him if that was the usual reaction he got when he saved someone's life. "Yes. Vampires have a bad rep."

"So long as you're helping my niece, I'm all right with you being whatever you need to be. I'm leaving my house now. I'm not telling her mom until I'm positive it's her." Brian asked her if she was usually so cautious. "You have no idea."

It was the longest drive of her life. Twenty minutes cut down to fifteen wasn't bad, but she wanted to get there in one piece. As soon as she walked into the ER, she stopped at the desk. Whatever was going on, CJ had a feeling that somehow it was her fault.

~*~

Brian watched the two women. CJ had called her sister when Rachel was taken to surgery. Her voice was calm, and even though she'd not shared the information with him, he knew that CJ was blaming herself for her niece being hurt. Pfeiffer, he assumed when they hugged, came in just as he was going to try and leave them to their family. The much younger woman hugged her as well. He knew they were all related by the way they looked like clones of one another.

"Don't leave." He shook his head at CJ and said he couldn't add anymore than he already had to the police. "I understand. You did save her life. You have no idea how much that means to all of us."

He could have told her more than he had the police. Brian could have told her that he had the scent of the two men that had beaten the young lady. The place where her car had been run off the road, and the woman trying to get away from them. However, he didn't. Being involved at all was something he didn't feel comfortable about. But when he got to Bancroft's, he was going to tell him everything, including who the men were and how he'd killed them both. There was evidence, too, that they had *thought* they had the woman in front of him. CJ was wanted by a lot of unsavory people.

"I just happened to be in the right place at the right time." She pointed to her lip and said he had a little spot on him. Licking away the drop of blood, he smiled at her. "You're taking this very well for not knowing about my kind."

"I know a great deal about your kind. I don't believe I've ever met a vampire before, but...." When she looked around, he did as well. But instead of talking to him about it, she pulled him into the ladies' room. After checking each stall, she locked the door. "Do you happen to know a person by the name of Bancroft? I'm not sure if that's his last or first name. Wait, don't answer that. I doubt you were going to anyway, but don't answer. If you happen to come across him at any point soon, you should tell him a task force is being put together that is hoping to kill him off."

"Do you happen to know why? I mean, if I ever run across him in my lifetime, he might well ask me the same question." She nodded. This time she put out her hand and put a thumb drive into his palm as they shook hands. He nodded. "You just happened to have this on you in the event you found a vampire?"

"No. I have that on me all the time. If it were

to fall into the wrong hands, I wouldn't be found." Brian wondered what was on the drive and why she trusted him with it. "I can see you have thousands of questions. I do, as well. However, I can tell you this much here. I work for different companies by putting security systems in place. Firewalls if they want them. Sometimes it's only putting in a program that gets employees to clock in and out. With that, I can walk around in their brains, the ones on their computer. I came across that three days ago when I was working for an office."

"And you trust me with this. Why?" She told him she had no idea why, but she *did* trust him. "I have your scent now, CJ. If you're trying to fuck me over, I'll hunt you down and kill you."

"All right." She put out her hand again. "Would you please have a connection to me? I know how that works. You'll be in my head all the time. I would like that, so if I am in trouble or I find out something more, I can give you fair warning. Also, if I'm taken, which I think will happen daily, then perhaps you can save me as well."

"Again, I don't understand this. For whatever reason, I have the same sort of trust with you." She nodded and stood there. "All right, CJ, I'll take your blood, but you must take mine as well. That will give us a tighter connection so that I will also know where you are if you're taken."

"I'm all right with that. However, if it comes to a choice for you to save me or my family, they're to be at the top of your list. I won't have anything happen to them because I'm good with computers." He said he would do that for her. "Promise me, Brian. I can't stand the thought of someone harming them. But they will to get to me. Promise me."

"I promise that if there is a time I can either save you or your family, I will save them." He grinned, not even bothering to hide his fangs. "However, I will do my damndest to make sure you're safe as well."

She left the bathroom before he did after they exchanged blood drops. Pulling shadows around him, he waited until someone came in and left when the door was still open. Brian didn't know what to do now. If he stayed here, CJ and her family would be safe. If he went to talk to Bancroft, he'd be able to figure out what was going on with the drive. Smiling to himself, he thought of the perfect plan.

Hello, Bancroft. I'm in serious need of you to send someone here to Mercy Hospital. I have something for you. He asked him why he couldn't come. *I don't know precisely, but your name has come up attached to someone wanting to kill you.*

I see. Do you happen to know who this person is? He explained to his oldest and dearest friend what had happened in the last few hours. *Okay. This woman, do you know her name? Anything about her?*

Her name is Circe Jane Montgomery. She goes by CJ. I do know that she works on computers. However, we have exchanged blood, and she is someone that I instinctively trust. I have no idea why, but I know she's not lying to me and that she's scared of being killed. Bancroft told him that Kelly wanted to go get whatever it was he had. *Thumb drive. And make sure Kelly isn't alone. I don't know what's on this drive, but they might have some knowledge of her as well.*

Brian, you're scaring me a little. He told him he was sorry, but he thought this was important. *I agree with you, but it doesn't make me any less afraid. I'm an old vampire, and to think that someone out there thinks they can kill me makes me wonder what sort of lengths they're willing to go to.*

By the time Kelly and Donald showed up, Rachel was out of surgery and in recovery. The other women were with her. CJ told him she was going to make a full recovery, but it was going to be a long road.

"I have someone that is going to take the drive with them. I'm going to stay here to make sure the four of you are safe. I don't know who might be coming to get you, but you're vulnerable here. Too many people coming and going all the time."

"Thank you." She didn't say anything for a few seconds, and he decided this woman knew a great deal more than she was letting on. *I was just thinking about something. Something that I got back from one of my clients last night. He said he didn't get the program I sent him. However, it was opened, as was the email. I wonder if his computer has been compromised. It can't be mine. I'm too good to let that happen. But what if someone is trying to get to me through some of the people I work for? Then, in turn to Bancroft?*

I know squat about computers at the level you seem to have. But I'd say if they were trying to get to Bancroft — who I do know, by the way — then they'd do whatever they can to make you a target. She told him that was what she was just thinking. *I know you love your family, CJ, but you shouldn't stay around them. The farther you are away from them, the safer they can be. Also, I'm going to send someone to your home when your family leaves.*

My Grannie. I forgot about her. Can you make sure she's safe as well? He said he would. CJ told him where she was and the code word to give to her if she had to leave with someone other than her. *I've left nothing to chance, I thought, but right now, I feel my life unraveling at a high rate of speed.*

I'm going to do my best at keeping you all safe. Even Bancroft will if it comes to that. Can you tell me, through our link, what is the reason they want to kill my friend? She was thinking. It was tempting to look into her mind to see what all she knew, but he also knew to do that would put a wedge between them and their trust for each other. *You don't have to if you don't think —*

Bancroft is a lord of a kiss. I'm not sure what that is. A kiss, I understand, but not what him being a lord is. Several hundred years ago, Bancroft purchased a large chunk of land that is now worth billions. His wife is human and corrupted. Their words, not mine. Their plan is to kill him and take his wife. I know that doesn't sound like much of a reason to kill him, but that's only one part of the information on the drive. That drive holds information about six different companies and their mentioning of Bancroft. He asked if that was the worst. *Not even close. They want to take him to a lab and drain his blood to give to the highest bidder. They believe by draining him and selling his blood, they'll have humans all over the world wanting some of it to live forever. I'm not sure, but I don't think that'll work. But then, that's one of the other plots. The worst one I came across was a satanic group that wishes to use him to call forth the devil, so they can be one with their god.*

Christ. CJ told him that she thought so as well. *All right. I've given the drive to Kelly, and Donald, the man that came with her, is going to pop her home. I'm not leaving here until you decide what you wish to do.*

I guess you're right. I have to leave. He said he was sorry. *As am I. They're all I have, and I don't want to leave them.*

He didn't tell her it might not do any good to leave them. If they knew about her family, they'd used them no matter where she was. Thinking along those lines, he thought he was going to need more help than he'd first thought. They needed to just disappear, the entire family.

He looked at Kelly when she sat down next to him. Telling her everything through the link they had because of her being mated to Bancroft, he also told her what he wanted to do. Hide them. All of them.

All right. Let me make a couple of calls, not to my work. As yet, we don't know how these people are affiliated with other people. We can put them in our home, and they'd be safe for a while, but I think they need to be hidden deeper than that. Brian thanked her for going to so much trouble for him. *You would have done the same for us.*

Yes. Without a second thought. She smiled at him, and he felt his face heat with *embarrassment. I walked right into that one, didn't I?*

I won't hold it against you. But I'm glad to know that, even though we've only just met, you'd take care of me. Okay. You and Donald stay here, and I'll see what I can do from home. For now, we'll just have them as guests at our home. I think that it will be safer than at their home. By the way, did you kill the men that beat up her sister?

Yes. She said she thought so. They'd found their bodies an hour ago. *I was pissed off that they'd hurt someone. They really did a number on her too. Without my blood, she would have surely died before I could get her to the hospital.*

I'm assuming neither of them are your mate. He explained to her the feelings he had concerning CJ. *Is that something important? What I mean is, is she one of the others' mates? I'm still learning things here.*

I never thought of that, but she could very well be. He thought of how the other vampires he knew were protective of women. *It could also be that we've been ingrained with the need to protect all females. I know I was sort of beaten over the head with how to protect the women of any species. We can test that theory when Donald gets back.*

It certainly would make her safer if she was one of their mates. She stood up and hugged him. *Donald is going to pop me home, then come back. I'll let you know what we find on the drive. We're going to only open it with a laptop without any access to other computers. Perhaps we should send someone to their home to clean it out.*

Good idea. She hugged him again, and Donald appeared behind her. *Don't forget to let me know. I like this woman, and I don't want anything to happen to her family. I've sent someone after Grannie too.*

After Kelly left and Donald returned, the two of them sat in the lobby of the ER and watched people. It was somewhat fun. They made up a game together where they would guess why they were there before looking. CJ reached out to him to let him know that her niece was in her room now. After getting that from her, Donald and he walked up the stairs to the second floor and waited for them there. In less time than he thought it should have taken them, the Montgomery family was sitting with them. Looking over at Donald, he asked him what was wrong.

Nothing. He asked him a second time but asked if one of the women was his mate. *Yes. I'm thinking it's the one walking around. But they're all so close together I'm having a hard time figuring it out. They smell the same.*

I'd not mention that if I were you. I don't know how a woman's mind works, but if you tell her she smells like other women, I'm sure you might lose your head. He nodded but kept watching the four of them. *This is good, right? I mean, whatever one you are mated to, you can be happy in knowing that they're all right as humans.*

Laugh it up, Brian. This only means you might be next.

Teasing his friend was fun. Brian thought he might be the only one to welcome a mate into his heart. He was looking forward to it more than he had anything for a long time.

Convincing the women wasn't nearly as difficult as they thought it would be. They knew that CJ wouldn't have told them it was dangerous if it wasn't. The fact that one of them had been hurt badly helped to persuade them as well. Taking them home one at a time. CJ and Rachel were the last to leave. It was then that Donald knew which one was his mate. He didn't know which one of them was taking it harder, either.

Chapter 1

Pfeiffer was enjoying this showdown of sorts between her sister, CJ, and the big man, Don, that seemed to be just as pissy about their status to each other. Not that she wouldn't jump to her defense if it came to that, but Donald was having a difficult time getting CJ to even speak to him. She told him, in no uncertain terms, that she wasn't going to get into it with him now, whatever that meant to either of them.

They'd been staying at the home of Kelly and Bancroft for the past few days. Rachel was getting better daily. She had a lot of stitches on her face and body, she was dealing with a lot of broken ribs, and her wrist was sprained. All things that she, as Rachel's mother, could live with so long as her daughter was all right.

Pfeiffer didn't know how she was ever going to repay the man that had saved Rachel's life. Without his lifegiving blood, Rachel would surely have died. Brian had told her, several times, that it wasn't anything for him to have helped Rachel. She also knew from Kelly that the man had destroyed the men who had hurt her. Not killed, but destroyed them. She shivered whenever she thought of that.

"Are you listening to me?" Shaking her head no, she smiled at her sister. "I asked you if you thought you were going to be all right here while I'm gone. I have to get this figured out, and if I'm around the three of you, it's only going to cause you more trouble."

"I don't want you to leave me. None of us do. But I understand that in order to get to the bottom of why they're hunting for you, you have to keep us safe." She glanced at Don as he asked them to call him, then back at her sister. "Are you going to take Don with you? I'd feel a great deal better about you leaving me if you were to do that."

"It doesn't seem I have much of a choice. He's fucking attached to me like glue." She looked at the handsome man, then smiled. "Maybe whoever is after me will take this out of my hands and take him instead."

"I'm pretty sure you know I can hear you. Also, I doubt very much that anyone would mistake you for me. You're much prettier, as well as very vocal about what you need and want." He grinned, and Pfeiffer was sure that whatever came out of his mouth was going to embarrass CJ again. "Are you like that during sex? Demanding and such? I'd think that would be one place I'd welcome you being so bossy. However, just so you know, I think I could make love to you and never have enough."

"Don't you have someone else to bother?" Donald said he didn't. "Well, I have work to do. And I can't do it with you breathing down my neck all the time. Go outside and get a tan or something. That might take care of my issues."

"You want me to die? So soon? Well, I'd say that isn't very nice, but so far, you've not really been nice to me." He seemed to think about that. "I haven't been all that nice to you either, but then, you've been sniping and biting at me since I found out what you were to me."

"When will it get through that thick head of yours that I don't want to be your mate?" He moved — or at least that's what Pfeiffer assumed he'd done when he was suddenly standing in front of her sister. "What are you doing? Back off."

"Not yet. I want to prove to you what you are to me." She said she didn't need this. Pfeiffer stood up, ready to protect her sister if she needed it. "I won't hurt her. I promise you on my life that I will do nothing to ever harm either of you."

"I think I understand that, but she doesn't play fair when she's cornered." Just as she finished saying that to Don, CJ moved, and Don ended up on the floor holding his groin. "I tried to tell you that. She's not used to being pushed. You might want to remember that in the future."

"I will."

Before she could understand what he was going to do next, CJ was on the floor with Don and held with her hands above her head. Her legs were on either side of Don, and that was when Pfeiffer decided she needed to leave them to this. They'd either kill one another or not. She couldn't do anything to help either of them.

"I was just coming to find you. I have some things I believe you can help me out with." She loved the older woman. Even though she looked the same age as Pfeiffer, she'd been told that she was very old. Gwyneth told her she was getting things worked out in the dining room. "I can't stand to be in the office for too long. It's just not me. But the way they've had the dining room set up, it's a wonderful place to work."

She looked at the mess on the table. It caused all kinds of havoc with her OCD. To her, if it wasn't in order, you weren't going to get things done in a good way. But she sat down and sat on her hands. It was just too much to look at, so she focused all her attention on Gwyneth.

"I'm to understand that at one time you were an accountant." She nodded and told her she had to leave the firm when she'd taken ill. "Yes, I've heard about that as well. I want you to know that I know that feeling. That you can't go on without your other half. I'm sorry if that's too blunt to you, but I'm sure you've come to understand that with vampires in the house, we don't take much in the way of chances about allowing people to be close to us."

"Robert was my husband. When he died, he took a great part of me with him. If not for CJ and my daughters, I might well have ended my life." She looked out the window as snow began to fall in large flakes. "He had cancer. No one caught it in time, so by the time they found it, he was too far gone for help and was dead the next week. I miss him with every breath that I take."

"My husband was my world, too. We took in Banny to raise not long after his parents were killed. Nasty business back then when they found a vampire. But after my Bancroft was killed too, it was all I could do not to join him. Banny kept me focused in the here and now. Along with his friends. You'll meet them all soon enough. But back to this help I need." She grinned at her, and Pfeiffer grinned back. "I can tell you want to get this organized. You've already taken one of the piles and fixed it for me."

She had. Even without knowing it, Pfeiffer had taken one of the piles of paper and put them in date order. It embarrassed her to no end that she'd been so rude. She told Gwyneth she was sorry.

"Don't be. I'm glad to see you know your stuff. However, I need these things not just in date order, but also by company. You see, this is the paperwork I got when I took over the job as head of the school board. It seems to me that a great deal of the funding raised for the elementary school is missing. Then there is the high school, as well as the preschool program that is in place." Pfeiffer, now that she knew she could nodded as she pulled another pile to her to organize. "I'm looking to have this information in a week if you can do that. I want to see if I can add to the sentencing of the little prick that was trying to make a profit off some of the lands the kids are now using for an educational outdoors program."

"We had that when I was in school." She was starting on the third pile of just putting them into date order. Then she'd work from there in getting them into business order. "I loved it. It's where I got my need to make jellies and jams when I can. Oh my, I have some at the house that I should go and get."

"You stay here, and I'll send one of the men over to get it. Anything else you might need as well. Pfeiffer, there are some really dangerous men looking for you to come home so they can take you to get to your sister. She told you that, didn't she?" Pfeiffer said she'd forgotten for a moment that they were on the run. "Not on the run, honey. Don't think of it like that. What you are is getting to know your new family members. If the two in the other room ever come to terms with what is going to happen to them once they fall in love."

"She was hurt once. It's been a long time, four years now, but she was dating this lovely man, or so we thought, and CJ was ready to get married to him. The two of them seemed to be such a couple that everyone who saw them could tell they were a perfect match." Gwyneth sat down and asked what had happened. "A week before the wedding, two men showed up at her house and said they were with the Feds. I was at her house then, or she might well have been arrested too. But they said they were looking for Peter Smirnoff. We didn't know who that was until they showed us a picture of Mike James, the man she was to marry. They went on to tell her that he'd been on their most wanted list for a very long time, and they thought he was only marrying her for her computer jobs. Turns out, she'd been smart enough to lock her things up without him being able to get to them since they met. Good thing too. Not that he'd have been able to get into her computer — she's that good at what she does — but he'd been trying very hard."

"So she was left holding the bag, so to speak." They both turned when CJ said it had been more than that. "I'm sorry. This is very rude of me to ask about your life when you're perfectly fine to answer on your own."

"It's fine. This is what I was just explaining to the idiot here. Why I have no desire to take on another person that is going to demand I do things his way. I hadn't really realized that until after he was arrested — that it wasn't just that he loved me, but he'd ordered me to love him. I don't have any heart left to love anyone. Just my family." Pfeiffer watched Don as she explained the rest of what had happened. "I was humiliated when he was taken away. Not by anyone that I knew, but he put it out there that I was a double agent working for several countries that were paying me well for what I knew. What he'd not counted on was the fact that we had nothing. Less than nothing. My mom was still alive then, and we were all living with her in the same home. There wasn't any evidence to back up his story. However, our lives were looked through so hard that it was difficult to even get a home loan for either of us. Much less a car loan. We'd been red-flagged, they told us."

"But you're thriving now." Pfeiffer said they were, but not by much. She told Don that if they had one large or even medium-sized issue, they'd be back to nothing again. "I can and will help you with that if you need it."

"We're not going to be on your list of charities. Have you listened to a single thing I've said to you?" Don told CJ he was talking to her sister at the moment, not her. "She's fine. I have a job that is paying well."

"You do, honey. And I love you for it. But with Rachel out of work right now and Sally being here with us, the income we did have nearly dried up." Pfeiffer knew she was poking the bear with her sister, but she looked at Don. "You could help us? I'd pay you back for whatever you deem a good interest rate. I've no way to work on the things I do and put a little by for the off chance of an emergency. Even staying here, we're still going to have to pay the taxes when they come due. Also, there are the other little things that happen when you're as broke as we are all the time."

"I can understand that very well. But something you need to remember, even if your sister is ten kinds of stubborn, is that you're my family now too. All of you, as soon as I met CJ, became my responsibility. I know that sounds old-fashioned, but I sincerely mean it when I tell you I will do everything in my power to keep you safe and without the stress of being without funds." She told him she wasn't his mate. "But you're her sister. And that alone means you're just as important to me as she is. And your daughters and Grannie. Who, I might add, is being much more cooperative than CJ is."

"Because she thinks you're the cat's meow. Whatever the hell that is supposed to mean." CJ sat down and looked as if she was going to cry. In all the years they'd been living together, she'd not once see her sister looking so defeated. "I lost my job this morning. The company I was working with on the program design fired me. In turn, several of the other companies I'm working for did the same thing. It's as if someone has put a black mark by my name, and I can't even get a job designing logos right now. I can't find out who it was because I can't get into my computers here. The Internet service here isn't secure enough for me to chance looking into anything."

"I can help you with that." CJ looked at Don, and there was such hope there on her sister's face that she was sure that Don couldn't have not noticed it. "Did you know that Kelly works for the Feds? She's been working for them for a while now and has a very secure network in the basement here. I could ask her if you could plug into it. Not that I think she'd have a problem with you doing that without asking, but I'd like to do that for you."

"Why?" Don asked CJ what she meant. "Why would you do this for me when you know I'm as stubborn as a mule and that I've turned you down every time you open your mouth about us? Which there isn't one."

"Because you need to figure this out, and I can help you with it. I'm a nice guy when you let me be. You've been bitching and fighting with me at every turn. I'm not going to hurt you in any way, shape or form, CJ. I swear to you that my only intentions right now are to make you happy and to keep everyone here safe." She told him, and Pfeiffer knew, that she'd not meant to be a bitch, but that she'd not been happy for a very long time. In fact, she told Don she wasn't sure how to be that way anymore. "I'm sorry for that. I truly am. But I can take some of the burden off you if you'd allow me to. I won't touch you until you want me to. I promise you that."

Instead of saying anything more, CJ got up from the table and left them there. Don started to go with her, but Gwyneth told him to wait for a little bit. Don looked at her and asked if he'd said something wrong to her.

"Don't promise her anything you have no intention of making come to fruition. She trusts that everyone who uses that word is only saying what they think she wants to hear. As I said, she's been hurt. Not just by Mike, but by a lot of people." Pfeiffer looked at him then and told him something she knew she shouldn't. "You'd be blown away by how many people owe her money. I've seen the invoices she sends out and how they're past due, some of them for the past few years of nonpayment. Not your fault, and I'm sure she knows that too, but promises mean nothing to her after being burnt so many times. Even our mother made promises that she never intended to keep. Grannie, I think, is the only person in this world that she trusts more than she does even herself."

"Do you have a list of the people who owe her?" Pfeiffer said she did. "I'd like it, please. Not that I'll go behind her back, but I can check out the reason they're not paying her. It might be something as simple as they're having money issues. I don't believe that, not for this long past due, but I would like to see what I can find out about each of the companies."

She wrote down the names she could remember. There were a lot more, she told him, but she didn't know all their names. When she handed what she could remember over to him, she put her hand over his.

"She won't be happy with either of us if you fuck this up. And while she might not be able to hurt you herself, you can bet that I won't have any qualms about selling my soul to someone to have your throat ripped out. Do you understand me? She's my baby sister, and I won't have you treading over her heart so you can get a good lay." Don nodded, then smiled at her. "Why on earth do you find that to be funny?"

"Grannie said the same thing to me not an hour ago. What she also told me was that if I fucked around and didn't make her fall in love with me, and soon, that she'd castrate me. I believed her, and now you. But I won't hurt her if I can help it. Never physically. I might hurt her by helping her, but I don't think that is what you mean." She told him it wasn't. "Then good. We're on the same page." He stood up and didn't leave right away but looked to the doorway where CJ had gone. "There will be money enough to keep you from worrying by the end of the day if you'll give me your information. Also, you should know that I, too, have been hurt, but not by a woman. My father. I'll tell you about it someday. But for now, thank you for trusting me with this. You've no idea how much this means to me."

"See that you don't fuck it up." He said he'd not then kissed her on the forehead. Looking at Gwyneth, she asked if she'd just made it worse. "I don't want either of them hurt, but if she can have someone love her, a forever love, then I'll help as much as I can."

"Don is a good boy, Pfeiffer. One of the best, next to my grandson. When he says he'll do something, you can bank on it unless something else comes along to keep him from doing it." Pfeiffer said she could understand that. "Good girl. Now, do you need anything from me to get the rest of this project finished up?"

"No. Just leave me to it, and I'll have them organized in no time." Most of it was already done, Gwyneth pointed out as she left the room. "I work when I'm stressed."

Gwyneth was still laughing when she left the room. These were an odd bunch of people. They all laughed at the strangest things. Pulling another pile to her, Pfeiffer got to work on it. She didn't know what she was in for, but for now, she was doing something she loved. Organizing.

~*~

Don just sat on the deck when he noticed that CJ was talking. It took him several minutes to realize she wasn't speaking to herself as he had thought but to a faerie. He wondered then how she'd ended up with a faerie. It must be a wonderful story. Watching her, he saw her turn to look at him before she finally stood up. That was when he noticed that not only did she not have on a coat, but no shoes either. She sat in the other chair, and the faerie sat on his bent knee.

"I'm Cody." Don told him he was happy to meet him. "Thank you, sir. I have some information I can share with you. It's about Ms. CJ here. She's got a man looking for her. Not a company as I thought at first, but a single man. I've told her that—"

"Why are you telling me, Cody, and not my mate?" He glanced over at CJ, then back at him. "Has she told you she's not speaking to me, or—?"

"No, I didn't tell him shit. He's telling you so I can think about what he said. But if you want to think everything revolves around you, then I'll tell you.

The person who is looking for me is a vampire. Old, but that's about all he knows. Cody also told me I don't know him." Don asked if she knew why he was looking for her. "Bancroft. This vampire, who I wasn't aware of him being a vamp, is one of the many people I knew were looking for the other man, but I don't know why. Again, because of the Internet situation."

"What's his name?" She told him. "I've heard that name before. I can ask around to the other vamps here and see what they might know about Parker. I think his name was associated with a kiss that was raided some years ago that was killing humans for the pleasure of it."

"That would be him. And in the event you aren't aware of it yet, I'm the one that reported them to the council. To be honest with you, I had no idea anything had been done to it until just this morning when I was speaking to Gwyneth. She told me that Bancroft hadn't done anything then, as he wasn't the lord of the vampires." Don asked her how she'd found the kiss. "I used to work for the council finding nests — what I was told they were called — for them to clean them out. I did wonder what had happened to the men that would ask for help. I guess Lord Vampire is in charge of it now."

"He is. But I'm betting that if asked, he had no idea that you were helping them out. It seemed to me and a great many others that they were only out for the profit of having their jobs. Robbing from other vamps." She looked at him and told him what she'd found out. "Ah, so they would call you to find them then clean them out. Of not just vampires, but the things they had stashed away too. That sounds like them."

"Should I offer him my services? I mean, it's not that hard to figure out once you know what you're looking for." He asked her how she knew it was a nest. "I can see them going in and out of the building at certain times of the day. But there are no heat signatures around them unless they'd just fed. Which, it occurred to me just now, wasn't all that often. What does that mean?"

"It could have been because they were old. But I'm doubting that. Older vampires, like me and Bancroft, have been around long enough to know that nests aren't the way to go. They'll get you killed faster than anything." She looked out across the yard. "I'm sure that you asking to help Bancroft will be something he'd like. He's new to this lord stuff, but you can bet he is really good at it."

"I'm supposed to offer you a faerie." Don asked her why she thought he'd need one. Not that he was turning her down, but why. "About ten years ago, just after my sister's husband died, I was grieving in private. I didn't much like Robert—I thought him incredibly lazy. But Pfeiffer loved him and his children.

So I tolerated him. Anyway, while I was hiding out, I came across something I didn't understand. It was a woman that was fading in and out of focus. I got closer to her, just to see if my eyesight was going when she turned to me. She was bleeding badly from a wound at her throat. I didn't even take a second to consider the consequences of my actions and offered my wrist to her. Then I hid her out in the building I owned and kept an eye on her."

"The faerie queen, I'm guessing." She nodded at him without looking in his direction. "She was gone from her castle for about a week when it happened if I remember correctly. No one knew where she'd gone, and some were worried she'd been harmed. However, when she returned, she never told anyone what had transpired, but she was a good deal more cautious after that. I'm assuming she repaid you in some way that pissed you off."

"Yes. I won't even ask you how you knew that. But she did repay me with magic. A good deal of it, as a matter of fact. And she gifted me Cody, who has been with me since. We're good for each other." He asked her if that was why he needed a faerie too. "I was speaking to her a little while ago. She comes to see me when she feels the earth move. I guess it did when you were holding me down."

"I felt it. Did you?" She told him she might have been too pissed off to have noticed. "Does she want to see me?"

"She's here now. And she told me she knows you and the other vampires already." He nodded, and when the wind picked up a little and small sparkles of light began to curl around like a small air eddy, he stood up and got down on one knee. "You do know what you're doing is going to piss her off, don't you?"

"Yes. He knows." He glanced up at Melisandre when she spoke. "Get up, you old fool, before I put a hex on you that will make it so you never will be able to satisfy your new mate."

"You don't have to worry about that one. I'll do it if he gets the least bit frisky with me." Melisandre sat down on one of the chairs, and so did Don. "I was just telling him how you were hurt."

"I'm sure she played down her part in saving me a great deal. What did she say that she found me and gave me some blood? That would be like her to do that. However, I was there, and I know she not only found me, but she found me with several men who thought it would be a good deal of sport to rape me. I didn't have the strength to fight them off, as I had only just made the flowers for spring open. It took a great deal out of me. She not only killed all six of them but also made sure I was put in a safe place to rest. Six men, without so much as a weapon to her name but her wits." Melisandre looked at CJ. "She has been gifted with magic, Don, but she's never used any of it.

A great deal of it was given to her by many creatures of the earth too. It would have saved her a great deal of grief from the bastard that tried to marry her."

"She's proven to me that she's very capable of taking care of herself. With or without magic." Don watched the two of them. He wondered if either of them knew how much they looked alike. "I'm going to ask this because if I don't, it will haunt me. Melisandre, what is CJ to you?"

The smile from the queen was very telling. It was also sort of scary. The connection between the two of them might not be anything at all, but for some reason, Don thought there was a great deal more to it than just one helping the other.

Chapter 2

Fergus needed something to do. If he didn't find a job of some sort soon, he was going to have to go back west and miss seeing his daughter. Not that they were terribly close, but she was coming to him for things now. However, none of it was keeping his mind or his hands busy. Going to find Don, he sat in his office for several minutes before the man looked up from the device, a computer he was staring at.

"I'm trying to find us a home. All I think about is that I have a mate, and I get sidetracked very easily." His smile seemed to consume his entire face. Ah, to be in love again. "What can I do for you, Fergus?"

"I can write a check." That sounded silly even to his own ears. "I'm sorry. I'm very bored. And you know as well as I that being bored is dangerous for men such as us. Do you, by chance, have anything for me to do? Physically would be better, but even a mental challenge is better than I have right now."

"I have several projects going right now. Two of them are things I've been asked by Bancroft and Kelly to do, and one of them is something I've been mulling around for the last few days. What do you know about construction?" He told him that several times in his life, he'd been in construction for a time. "Good. Even if it was a while back, it's more than I have right now. I need to see what sort of work it would take to change out the school that has been sitting idle for decades. Should it be taken down? Can I reuse it the way it is? I need someone that knows more than I do to go there and see if it would be cheaper to rip it to the ground or renovate it into a greenhouse flower shop. I think the need is there, especially for the greenhouse. And I found out recently that my mate is a cousin to Melisandre."

"I thought she'd been created. I mean, isn't that the way it is for queens and kings of the other world?" Don explained it to him. "I had no idea that Melisandre was the second queen. So Melisandre's mother is a sister to the father of CJ. What about her sister?"

"They're not related. Not by blood anyway. CJ knows, but her sister Pfeiffer doesn't. Apparently, when there was an upheaval in the other world, CJ was brought here to this world to be safely hidden away in the event she was needed to take over the other world for the queen. If she was hurt or incapacitated in some way, they had someone that could hopefully fill the spot. It turned out all right, but they forgot about CJ being with a human family, and she has been here since." He asked about the parents. "That's the thing. When Pfeiffer's parents were alive, they traveled a great deal. Then one time, when they came home with a baby, no one seemed to be confused or concerned about it. Pfeiffer, just like everyone else, thought CJ was their child and her sister. That's why there are a lot of years between them."

"And no one thought to figure this out? No questions were asked about the child, even after the years had gone by?" Don told him apparently not. "That is not only strange, but it seems a little cruel if you ask me. It's akin to what happened to my daughter. Someone changed Lizzy against her will, and this child was left behind with no one to help her with her magic." Fergus thought about it for a moment before speaking again. "You know, it must be hidden. Now that I think on it, I've never smelled magic on her."

"Neither have I. You will now. When Melisandre was here earlier this morning, she made sure that anyone around them knew CJ has magic." Fergus asked him about his portion of magic. "I've been marked."

Standing up, the young man took off his shirt. He had been marked, and it looked as if he was still getting markings put to his skin. His entire right shoulder and arm were marked with symbols and sigils that Fergus had not seen for a very long time. Getting a closer look at them, he could tell that some of it was written in faerie.

"It says you are to be protected at all costs. You are...hang on. It's been a while since I've had an opportunity to read this language. Let me see. You are the mate to the queen's family. Any children born of you and your mate will be cherished." Fergus looked at the next line of inked words. "I'm not sure, but it looks like this is telling me of the battles you've been in and how they turned out. Is CJ marked as well?"

"Yes. But apparently, she's had this mark on her back since birth. It was thought they looked like wings, but no one paid it much mind. But now that she's met me, she's been inked up as well. She's not all that happy about it either—the mate part bringing it out, not the markings." Don laughed. "I don't know if she's aware of it or not, but she's simply beautiful to me when she gets all pissy. It's like her eyes shine, and her hair seems to take on a life of its own. It's all I can do not to touch her."

"I'd not if I were you." Don asked him if he thought he was stupid. "No. But then men in love can do strange things when they find their other half. And you are in love with her, aren't you?"

"Yes. She has a spirit about her that draws me in. Makes me want to be a better person. She is also smart and funny, even when she's not trying to be." Fergus envied the man for just a moment. Then he thought of his own daughter and his love for her. "But we should be working. The building has been sitting for some time now. There was at one time a greenhouse on the land. The workings of it are still there, but the greenhouse itself is long since gone. I had an idea that, in addition to the plants and such, I could make up different settings for different types of plants. Also, classes on how to make sure a garden is healthy. This isn't my idea just so you know. It's brilliant, but Melisandre wants us to put something in that will keep the faeries busy all the time. CJ came up with the rest of it. Also a training ground for new faeries. Sometimes in working in the spring, she told us, training isn't possible. But with this and the greenhouse, it will be a good time to show them, and also to make it so that people plant more flowers in their yards. Something that we both know is needed."

"I can do that." Don told him he'd have a crew working with him. "Faeries, I'm assuming."

"They'll work in the evenings after the regular crew is gone. Mostly to plant the items that will sell. Also, they'll work on large planters and the like.

Putting them together so they will look good, as well as last much longer than ones a human would be able to put together at home. CJ told me they can do the clean-up as well but will stay hidden during the day in the event there might need a special project needed." Fergus was excited about this job. It sounded like something that would keep him busy for a long time. "Some of the little people will be living in the greenhouse—again, out of sight. The greenhouse will be open to the public as well. The rooms in the building, as I said, will be used for different types of plants. Also offices, as well as storage."

"It sounds like you have this all worked out. What happens if the building isn't worth it? I'm sure you have a backup plan." He nodded but didn't seem to like plan two. "It can't be all that bad, is it?"

"I'm not sure. I've been told all my life that faeries can do the work of a thousand men if given the chance. In this project, they want to go in and redo the entire building from basement to roof. I am against the idea. Not because of the faeries, but there are a great many men and women out of work right now. This would put a few more meals on the table that might not happen if there is no work for them." Fergus's respect for this young man doubled just then. Thinking of the people they were hoping to sell to and making sure they were all right as well. "I want to be able to help Melisandre, but not at the cost of putting people out of a job. Does that make sense?"

"Shifters would be able to do it as well and quickly. What if they worked together on this project? I know from speaking to some of the pack that roams the land hereabouts that they're not working as much as they'd like to. I'm sure something can be worked out for all the people involved." Don seemed to like that idea. "Put them in the same working area. Shifter with faerie. I know there are a great many other projects going on right now that can fulfill the needs of some of the humans without them being aware of the faeries."

"I like that idea. And the school is far enough out that no one would notice it being taken care of too quickly." He said that would work for him. "It will put more people to work, too. Thank you. That was really bothering me."

"It's all right. I know just how you feel when it comes to working with the humans as much as we can." They agreed on a wage for Fergus. Not that he needed the money, but he could and would donate it back to the projects that were going on, as he'd been doing. "I need to find me a place to live. I know you're working on that as well. So if you'd not mind finding me a home that I can live in, close to my daughter's home, I'd appreciate that."

"Yes, I will." Don grinned, and he had to smile back at him. "I can tell CJ that I'm looking for you and ask her what she thinks of the house while we're at it. She's working today, setting up the system to help with the inventory at the pantry. The donations are going a long way in getting food to shut-ins, as well as anyone that just needs a boost. And the car service is going so much better than we thought it would. It looks as if people are making a lot of friends with it too."

"Lizzy was telling me that the high school kids are getting involved with that part of it. They're getting to use a car that has been purchased for their use as a companion for the elderly." Don told him how the younger pups from the pack were visiting the shut-ins, too, to keep them company during the day. "That is brilliant. I think I could have used that a little when I was lonely. Just someone to talk to."

"It's the first time in my life that I'm enjoying working with humans. It had been so long since I trusted them not to stake me. It's scary and refreshing as well." Fergus told him it had taken him a long time to do that as well. "I still find myself keeping an eye out for trouble. I suppose that's a good thing. But since I've met CJ, it's a little less stressful."

"You should talk to either your mate or Melisandre. I do believe that one of your perks for being mated to CJ will be something along the lines of you being able to withstand more trauma to your body. Stakes and the like might not be a factor in you being killed anymore." Don asked him why he thought that. "Well, you sort of glow with this untapped magic. I'm not sure that's the right term for it, but you look like you have this bubble around you, just waiting for someone to take you on. Like a protective shield. I noticed it around CJ too when I saw her today."

"I'll write that one down too. I have a list of things I'm going to ask Melisandre when we have our meeting tomorrow afternoon. If you'd like to come to the meeting with us, that would be fine with me. We're meeting her in her castle. She said she'd feel safer there with what she has to impart to us all. Bancroft and the others have been given magic as well. There is no reason for me to think you might not have gotten some of it." Fergus told him he thought he'd like to do that. "Good. She's sending a guard to pick us up at noon. I'm not entirely sure what that entails, but we'll be transported to her kingdom from this house."

"I'll be here then."

As he made his way to the building he was to look at, several faeries joined him on his walk. Sometimes he was a little afraid of the little creatures. Not that he'd ever been harmed by any of them, but they were so tiny he was terrified of hurting one of them. The one that was currently sitting on his shoulder began speaking as they were nearing the building.

"The building is very old, not in our years,

but to the humans. It wasn't torn down when it was replaced because they had plans to turn it into a hotel. That never happened, as I'm sure you're aware. There was too much money to be sunk into it, so it was just abandoned. Another time it was thought to make a nice antique shop, with each room being for one of the renters. But that too fell through when it was discovered the building wasn't up to code for as many people as it would need to hold." Don asked him if he knew how bad of shape the building was in. "For its age, it's held up well. We have been told we could take charge of the clean-up. It was very dusty inside, and some unwelcome animals had gotten in. We took care of the clean-up yesterday. I do believe it will be easier to ascertain what needs to be done to it with all the filth gone. By the way, I forgot to tell you my name. I am called Pin."

"I'm Fergus. Nice to meet you, Pin. As for the cleaning up, I believe you're right on that." They entered the building in the front of the place. "I can see right now that it's going to need new windows and doors. These wouldn't keep a varmint out if he needed to get in out of the cold."

"I am relaying the information to one of the faeries that are able to write. She is making the list of things you find while looking around." Fergus thanked him. "We will make a good team, I think."

It took them well over four hours to look the

building over. It wasn't really in bad shape, as Pin had told him, but it was going to need a great deal of work. As he moved out of doors to look at where the greenhouse was supposed to have been, he wasn't the least bit surprised to find that someone had already installed it where he thought the old one had been. He asked Pin about it.

"Even as the building is being worked on, we can start on some of the trees that we'll be able to sell. Mistress CJ said she didn't care so long as we didn't go overboard on the project. It was quite an undertaking to make sure that the others didn't make the building too large. We have trouble with scale, you see." Fergus laughed and said he'd done a fine job. It was perfect. "Thank you, my lord. Coming from you, that is quite a compliment. I shall tell the others that we did a good job."

The rest of the day was spent going over the list of things that needed to be taken care of. The two of them worked on prioritizing the list into what needed to be fixed by a professional and ones that the faeries could work on now. The little creatures would just make it work by magic, and while it would be quicker, they did need to hire people for this project that needed an income. By five o'clock, he had a working list and was ready to go see the queen with the others tomorrow.

~*~

CJ had been to the castle before, of course. It was a place she would visit when she needed some downtime. That being said, this was a new experience for her, as there were others in the large room that she was sure were making her nervous. Or it could have been the fact that Don was there, asking her questions about her magic. She didn't know half the things he was asking her about, but the faeries were more than happy to give him all he wanted to know.

"Do I make you upset?" She looked at Don and wasn't sure how to answer him. "I can go back to the house should you want me to. I can learn what I need to know from one of the others."

"It's not you, but all of you. I know that sounds terrible, but I'm not really used to sharing space with people. Groups of them, anyway. When I work, I have my door locked, so I can be undisturbed. There is no phone in the room, nor a radio or television. I can work for hours in the quiet." She looked around the opulent room they were in. "This room is made for a large gathering of people, but it echoes too. I'm just not used to being here when it's so noisy."

"I understand that. I have been alone for a very long time myself. The only time I would enjoy company was when I came to be with Bancroft and his grandmother. Gwyneth used to welcome us all to her home with open arms. Sometimes it would be just too much for her, too, I believe. Vampires, for the most part, are solitary beings. However, we like a good party as well." He laughed when she frowned at him. "If we can get us a house that is just far enough away from the others that they can't just drop in, yet close enough that if we needed them, they're there for us, would that be the way to go?"

"I don't know anything about buying a house. I did have one when I was first out on my own. But I didn't really spend a great deal of time there. Just to work, for the most part, and sleep. I was with Pfeiffer and her family most of the time. More so when Robert died."

He asked her what sort of things she wanted in one, like a pool or even a large kitchen.

"I'm assuming you don't cook." He said he didn't, but like Bancroft, he did have staff when he was at his other home. "You have a home then. Wherever it is that you came from."

"Several, as a matter of fact. Property as well. I kept my eye on markets—it's something all of us do when we're starting out. Most vampires that are made have no money set aside. Nothing they can fall back on. But as a born vampire, I have invested well and buy up things I can foresee making a profit at some point if I wish to sell it off. It doesn't always work out, but enough so that I have a lot of ready cash, as well as things I can sell off for more." She nodded as she wandered around the room. Melisandre had been called away, and they were all waiting for her to return. "What's really bothering you? By the way, Fergus told me that you glow with magic. I never noticed it before he mentioned it. I couldn't see past your beauty."

"Yeah, sure." She moved to one of the walls covered in a map of the realm they were in. "I wonder what a human would think if they knew this was just a portal in the world's distance away from them. And that some of the animals they think aren't real are living here and having families of their own. The first time I was here, I nearly lost it when I was approached by a unicorn. He was my escort, and I spent a great deal of time looking around instead of paying attention to where he was taking me."

"Have you been here a great deal?" CJ told him only when she was summoned. "I bet that doesn't go over well with you. Someone having you come to them."

"Not really. But it was nice to come here to relax. I think Melisandre can feel when I'm stressing, and she'll call me here to do something for her and have me wait around longer than necessary. I never realized she was doing that until recently." She turned and looked at him. "I've known all my life that I was different than the others. I think there were times when Pfeiffer did as well, but she never said anything to me. Her parents never knew about me not being their child. Mom, what I did call her, was pregnant when they left on their travels, but she lost the child one night in a terrible storm. Melisandre switched me with their stillborn child, and they never knew the difference."

"I did wonder about that — how you were raised by them. It seems sort of deceitful a little. Don't you think so?" CJ told him of the things that were done for them. Things that they never knew about. "So they were compensated for taking care of you by having their finances taken care of. That was nice."

"It couldn't be too much. I mean, not millions of dollars, or someone would have figured out who I was — then worse, where I was." Don said that too was a good thing. "Yes. I suppose. As I said, it's been something I've been keeping to myself since I was old enough to realize things."

"Will you ever tell Pfeiffer?" CJ told him that was what was bothering her so much. She was afraid she'd be mad at her. "Doubtful she'd hold the circumstances of your birth against you. It's not like you had anything to do with it."

"Yes, but I've known. And I still said nothing." She moved around the room more. Then she and Don ended up in the receiving hall. "May I show you something? It's nothing huge, but it's a place I have come to love more than anything on the human side of my world."

"I'd love to see it." She took his hand into hers and led him to the back portion of the castle. When they slipped out a door she used to get to her special place, CJ made sure it was locked so no one would be able to follow them. "This is beautiful."

"Thank you. I created it when I was here. Just for me." There was a large pond that had a fountain in the middle of it. The fountain had no form other than it took on whatever popped into her head when she was out here. She wasn't surprised to see it become Don, with his body naked but for a loin cloth. "You can see your markings here. They're finished for now. However, they'll change when you or I do something that needs to be written down. I've had mine hidden away by magic for so long that I was surprised a little to see them appear. It means to my kind that we are truly mates."

"So you doubted it." She told him it was more like she had hopes of it being wrong. "You dislike the idea of being mated to me that much?"

"No. It's not that at all." She looked at the statue of him and then back at the man himself. "I'm not sure I can explain this well enough that it doesn't make me sound stupid, but we're different, you and I. I don't mean the fact that we're vampire to faerie. Not even the age of us. But you are a man of the world. I'm nothing more than a person who has lived in the same area, including here, all my life. I don't have any friends that aren't related to me. You have friends that would gladly lay down their lives for you. I know the women of your family, but we're not close. They have only accepted me because of you."

"You can't really believe that, do you? I know that Bancroft is in awe of you. The fact that you can find nests for him and tell him what is going on inside of them is something he is proud of for you. Kelly thinks you're the seventh wonder of the world." She asked him what he thought of her. "That you're the most beautiful creature ever born. That you're smart and snippy all rolled up into one fascinating bundle. I love the way your eyes blaze when you're upset. The way you stomp when you're thinking. You don't have the need to empty your head when you're thinking of something. You're brutally honest, which is wonderful to me. I know where I stand and how you feel, no matter what. When you say something to me, I know whatever it is, it's from your heart and not your mind. Also, when you have an issue, you have no trouble asking for help and making sure that when you have finished getting help, you thank the person for their part in it, as well as make sure they get credit. I could go on if you wish."

"No. That's enough." Looking around the pond, she told him things about herself that she'd never said to anyone before. "I can look into a home and other places while never leaving where I am. See the future on investments that I will put money into. So long as I share my wealth, it's all right with the magical world. It's been the only thing that has kept us afloat after Robert died. I couldn't do too much, as you can well imagine. People would have noticed things. If nothing else, humans are not happy if someone has more than they do. Robert was like that to the very end."

"I've done some investigating on him. Just to see if there were some policies out there that might have been overlooked. He wasn't employed much. And when he was, it wasn't for very long. The reason they had no insurance at the time of his death, and your sister is—well, was—paying that debt off is because he never took the time to work at one place long enough to get it."

"I told you once that I didn't care for him. That's not true. I hated him. He took advantage of Pfeiffer at every turn. You're right about his unemployment record. Robert couldn't hold down a job if he had a gun to his head. He wasn't lazy...he just felt he was above menial things like making a living. He would have gladly drained her dry of money and time. The girls and I were never a part of his life. Even though I'm about the same age as her daughters, she had them despite Robert telling her he didn't want them around. That having me there all the time was bad enough. Rachel and Sally didn't care for him either. They didn't hate him, but they didn't care for him."

Don sat down on one of the many benches she'd put in this area. She sat at the water's edge. "I don't feel guilty for not helping him to live longer. I think even Pfeiffer was sick of him by then. After he was dead, it was easier to help her out when she needed it. Which, after the girls left home to do their own jobs, I still lived with her. To keep her safe."

"Did you have trouble even though few knew where you were?" She nodded, then looked at him. "Something is holding you back from making a commitment to me, isn't it?"

"Yes. There are still people out there trying to locate me. They know I exist, but not where or who I am. If I were to commit to you, as you called it, you'd be in danger as much as my sister has been all these years. As well as the others. All of them would be targets to get me to blackmail Melisandre." She could tell he was thinking hard on that. "I can understand that it's a lot to take on. And so that you're aware of it, I can take your meeting me from your mind. At least the part where you will know that I'm your mate. I don't want any—"

She found herself on her back, him atop of her again. This time she didn't struggle but let him hold her. It might well be the closest she got to having him touch her. The look on his face was hard for her to read. Harder still for her to think that he might not care about what came with loving her.

"You've held this secret for long enough, don't you think?" She asked him what he meant. "Making sure that others around you are safe while you take on the ones who are after you all alone. You aren't alone anymore, CJ. You have me. An entire kiss should you wish it. I'm sure that even Melisandre would give you a company of warriors should you but ask. I'm here for you, love. Will be there beside you or in front of you when the time calls for it. You may well be able to take memories of you from me, but my heart will only beat for you. I will wonder forever, should you do that, who has touched me in a way that gives me such sorrow that I cannot find you, can't remember your scent or the touch of your skin. I might well not remember you, but this place in my heart that belongs only to you will wither and die when I cannot find you."

"Oh, Don. You have no idea what your words have done to me."

The magic around them seemed to wrap them up. A cocoon-like feeling made of love and happiness lifted them up higher and higher. When Don took her mouth, putting all his passion into the kiss, she knew on every level that he was all she would ever need from this day forward.

Chapter 3

Don wanted to make love to her, needed to feel her body next to his, a part of his own. To claim her as his mate. Not because it was written that was the way his kind took a mate, but because he wanted her, her heart and soul. Thinking of taking her back to the bedroom he'd been using, he heard his name called, then CJ's. Don snarled aggressively at the person.

"I am sorry, my lord, but the meeting is about to begin. It is imperative that you both attend." He told the man to go away. "I cannot. I have been sent to bring you to the meeting, and I cannot disappoint or go against my queen."

He looked down at CJ. She had the strangest look on her face—glazed eyes, her mouth turned up in a smile. When he leaned down to kiss her, she turned her head away. Pain shot through his heart as if she had actually staked him.

"If you kiss me right now, I'm going to come screaming your name, and then there is no way in hell we're going to make it to this meeting." She looked at him. "I kid you not, Don. I'm so very close to losing it that one touch, and I'm a goner."

Standing up, he felt like he was ten feet taller. The pain that had nearly doubled him over was now a good feeling, wrapping around his wounded heart and mending it. Pulling her up from the table, he pulled her to him, and with a quick kiss on her nose, he moved to the door to open it. He nearly let his beast go when he saw what was on the other side.

"We're coming." The guards were standing there, their weapons out and their body armor so bright it was nearly blinding to him. CJ walked by them and into the room, but he stood his ground. Looking at the man in front, Don let his beast go long enough to realize that he and his men would surely die if they attacked him.

"I'm sorry, my lord." He pulled himself together then walked by the men. The man in charge stopped him with a hand to his shoulder. "We were not to harm you but to make sure you were not delayed because of someone holding you. I swear to you, it was never our intention of harming either you or the Lady CJ."

"She's that important to you?" The guard looked

in her direction, then back at him before nodding and telling him that he was just as important now. "Why? What does she have that makes you think to come into a room with a vampire and his mate?"

"There are many that would take her to get to our queen. A great many more would lose their lives should that happen. The queen will stop at nothing to return her to her home should she be taken, but with you at her side, we all rest a little easier." The man, he told him his name was Daniel, smiled. "We didn't worry overly much when she was alone, my lord. She is what the queen calls feisty. Scary if you ask me, but we still will die for the two of you."

As he returned to the big room, he looked around again, this time with an eye on security. He could see guards where he'd not before. There were warrior faeries flittering above them. Some were standing in front of paintings, so they were camouflaged. The people walking around serving drinks and small snacks were armed. Even at the balcony, he could see men and women with a quiver of arrows at their back, their eyes on the people below them. Before he could look more, someone tapped him on the shoulder.

"Do you see any place where I am lacking, Donald the Warrior?" Don bowed before the queen, and she smiled at him. "When will you understand that I don't need that sort of treatment from you? You have been and forever will be my friend. And now you are my family."

"I will forever think of you as a friend as well, Melisandre, but first and foremost, you are queen of all faeries." He smiled at her when she frowned. "How about I only pay reverence to you when we are in a public setting? Then when we're alone, I'll try not to show you so much."

"If that is the best I can get from you, then I shall take it." They both looked where laughter came from the front. It was CJ and a group of small children. "When she comes here, they are the first people she asks after. They look forward to her coming as well. She brings them things to play with, and when she's able, CJ will sit and read to them until they go to bed."

"She tried warning me off. I was told she's hunted even now." Melisandre told him the magic she'd been given would keep them both safe. "I won't be bargaining for her life. If they have her and want you in some way, I will stop at nothing, and I do mean nothing, to keep the two of you safe."

"Thank you for that." She looked at him, and he could see fear there. "She is all I have in the way of family, Don. And like you, I would do anything to keep her safe. Having you as a mate, it will help her in many ways she's not thought of. But I do fear she will be hurt before she uses what is rightfully hers."

"The magic." She told him that was it. "If it will help her, I'll work with her on it. I'll also share with her everything I have."

"Good." She laughed. "I don't envy you that task. She isn't just stubborn. I do believe when the word is looked up, it has her description there, as well as her set face when she's upset."

"I'm all right with that because she is stubborn, but she's not stupid. I think if she got in over her head, she'd ask for help." Melisandre said he was right about that. "I'll talk to her after this meeting. I'm sure you're about ready to begin, aren't you?"

"Yes. You're not going to be any happier than her when you find out what you've gotten. Also, I would suggest someone talk to her sister, Pfeiffer. She will get a little of this as well because she too could be used as a way to get to us." He asked her why she was afraid of anyone getting to her. "There are people out there, in my realm as well as yours, that believe my magic is only for show. That I'm not needed anymore. With computers and the like, they believe they'll be able to do my job in less time and with less effort. Of course, they have no idea what sorts of things would cease to be if I were to disappear. You too would perish if not for the magic I put to the earth."

He wasn't entirely sure what that would entail until he was seated in the large room. Looking around, he saw the faeries there and tried to equate what they did with the flowers that would affect him. Then it hit him. There would not only be no more flowers but bees would no longer be supported. Gardens that fed the people he had needed to feed from would perish, and the people would starve. There would be no more animals either. Grass would wither and die. Even trees needing to be pollinated would die as well without the magic of the faeries that were a part of the queen's arsenal. Don didn't know what these other people were thinking. He realized he needed to do something to get the word out. Tell people that fucking with the queen would profoundly affect them all.

Don only half-listened to what Melisandre was saying. He would tune into what was going on for a few minutes and then go back to his thoughts about the world. Things, he knew, were going to end badly if someone didn't do something soon. Very soon. When CJ poked him in the ribs, he looked around, and everyone was staring at him. Standing up, he smiled to the group.

"I'm sorry. I was thinking about something that has come to my attention. The people we're worried about the need to be able to understand what they're doing by fucking with the queen and her job." CJ told him that was what they were talking about. "Good. Then I'd like to head up a program or something that would get the word out as to what happens to the world if there is no one to start the process of pollenation. Because essentially, that is what keeps all of us alive."

"You have it figured out yet?" He told Bancroft he was only just now thinking of the timeline of the death of the world as anyone knows it. "That's a pretty harsh way to put it. You believe that?"

Don explained to the group what he'd been thinking about, all the way through their lives ending with the demise of the world itself. He could tell by their faces that they hadn't thought of that either. That a simple thing like bees not being able to get to the nectar of the plants could end everything.

"I'm in. Also, you can count on anyone else you think you might need in the way of vampires. This is much more important than just a few trees dying off." Don thanked Bancroft. Everyone said they'd help as well. Melisandre hugged him tightly, then he sat back down.

"Now that we have the most important thing discussed, I'd like to go over the magic all of you have received. None of you will have lost whatever you were before this came to you. If you were a vampire before this, you will continue to be one. However, now you will be able to shift into anything, living or not." She looked at him. "Don, come up here, please, and I'm going to demonstrate on you."

He wasn't sure about this and told her so. After she called him a baby, he smiled at her as he bowed before her when she told him to behave. Then she told him to think of any animal, any of them, and shift.

All he could think about at that moment was a hawk. It was his favorite of all the creatures of the earth. It had beauty, poise, and killer instincts that rivaled his own. When everyone applauded, he took a moment to realize that he'd done it. He was a hawk.

Someone asked if he could fly, so he took to the air as if he'd been born to it. As if he knew exactly what to do to make it happen. Don was able to soar throughout the building and around the heads of the people below him. Stopping when all he wanted to do was go out into the fresh air, he landed before Melisandre, and this time felt the need to bow before her for what she'd given him. Even if he never flew again, it had been the best few minutes he'd ever felt.

"As you can see, whatever it is you're shifting to, you'll have complete knowledge of how to make the bird or anything do what is needed." She thanked him, and he shifted from the hawk to himself without any issues. He was also fully clothed in what he'd had on prior to shifting. "There are a few things I'd like to go over. I'm sure I don't have to tell you this, but you might well learn more by trying things than you will if I were to go over each bit of magic."

They spoke about things he'd been thinking about, things like helping Melisandre when she needed it. The queen told them about payment, which he sort of got lost in. His thoughts were mostly centered on the upcoming project he had to start.

By the time he was ready to get back home, he had so much going through his mind that he thought he might be better off carrying around a notepad and pen. CJ told him he could easily use his phone, but he'd never been that good with electronics and favored using a stationary phone instead. Mostly because he would forget where he put his phone and have to either replace it or retrace his steps for hours, only to give up.

When they were back at the house, he realized it wasn't nearly as late as he'd thought it was. He knew there was a time difference when going into the other realm — CJ had told him that. However, it was only two in the afternoon, and he asked CJ if she wanted to go and look at homes with him.

"Unless, of course, you wish to live with Bancroft for the rest of our days." She looked so horrified that he burst out laughing. "All right. I've been looking around for Fergus a place to stay and found a few that you might like. We'll need staff, and it's my understanding that we'll use faeries for that. Melisandre said it would be safer for all of us if we were to have them around more often."

"I've been looking as well. I didn't think of us living together when I started out. I had just decided I didn't want to live with Pfeiffer anymore. And after I have a talk with her about all this, she might not want to even live around here anymore either." He asked her if she really thought that. "I don't know. I think I'm hoping for the best but planning on the worst-case scenario."

"If it will help, I can go with you." She said she wasn't sure what would help. He hurt for her in this. "Whatever you need, I'm there for you. However, I'd not wait too long. She'll have magic. How much or even what she can do will be a surprise to her no matter how she finds out."

They decided to get it over with. First, they stopped by the home he'd been looking at and got out to look around. The realtor was going to meet them at seven tonight, so they wanted to get a little sneak peek at it now. He was blown away by what she'd thought of in a home for herself.

"According to the information, it has fifty acres around the house that is all good soil. Not that it would matter all that much. Once I moved in, it would have been very good anyway. The other faeries or I would have fixed that for me. Well, us, I guess." She read off the things she had on the place as he walked up to the circular front porch. It wrapped all the way around the house and was wide enough to have plenty of chairs for sitting. "There is a fishing pond out back. Also, a barn that I'm told needs to be repaired in places. It has electricity, as well as heat and air. The river runs through the property in several places, and there is a boat as well as a boat house that would be ours."

"I want it." They were laughing as they walked around the property. "The land back here, it is rich smelling. Also, it looks as if at one time there was an expansive flower and rose garden." He moved along the stone wall that led him to a large tree with several benches under it. "I'm sure this will be a beautiful setting come next spring."

The two of them walked around for about half an hour. Don was tempted to break into the place just so he could make sure the inside was just as impressive as the outside. CJ pointed out that if the house was shit, they could simply build. But he had a feeling that whoever had cared so well for the land had done so with the house as well.

"We'd better get going. I was thinking of taking my nieces and Pfeiffer out to dinner. You know, to sort of have her in a place where she won't make a scene. But that's not going to work with her. If she's upset, which doesn't happen all that often, she doesn't care who is around." They pulled up in front of the home Pfeiffer was renting for now and were greeted by a couple of dogs coming out to see them. Shifters, she realized. Big ones that seemed to know they weren't human and stayed back. CJ just didn't understand why she wouldn't just stay with them. It was much safer than living alone out here. "They were sent here by Melisandre, I'm thinking."

As it turned out, the dogs didn't take long to warm up to them. As they entered the house to see if they could talk to Pfeiffer, she met them in the living room with the most terrified look he'd ever seen on a woman's face.

~*~

Pfeiffer sat down on the couch. She hated the thing, really, but it was that, or she was going to go back home. It scared her to no end that while she was looking for something to snack on before her dinner, the carrot sticks and peanut butter appeared on plates. Plates that she knew she didn't own. Looking at CJ, she asked her to explain.

"Okay. How do you want this, Pfeiffer? Straight up or a little at a time." She wanted it slowly but thought she'd be better off getting it right up front. At least until she was overwhelmed. She told her that. "All right. I'm not really your sister. I'm a faerie."

Pfeiffer looked at Don, then back at CJ. After laughing just a little to let the tension she was feeling slide off her, she nodded. Then she told her what she knew.

"I've known that for years, CJ." Good, she thought. She'd thrown her off if the look on her face was any indication. "I knew you weren't my little sister when Mom and Dad came back, and you were...how should I put this? You were different. I saw you doing magical things that — Something has happened, hasn't it? Something important, and you've shared some of what you have with me. That's why there were carrot sticks on the table."

"Yes." CJ leaned back on the couch and looked at her. Pfeiffer took her hand into hers. "I thought for sure you were going to leave me here. That you'd be so pissed off that you'd never have anything to do with me again."

"That would be stupid. It doesn't matter that you aren't my blood relative—you're still the sister of my heart. I love you. Nothing is going to change that." She smiled at CJ. "Tell me why I have carrot sticks."

"You need to tell me why you're all hung up on carrot sticks first." Pfeiffer told her what had happened in the kitchen. "All right. That is something I didn't know you'd be able to do. There might be more. I'm not at all sure what you might have gotten. I can make you immortal, for one thing. And the girls."

"I know what that word means, but I have a feeling it's something entirely different when you tell me this." CJ told her it meant she could never be killed. By any means. "All right. And Rachel and Sally? They'll be the same?"

"Yes. As a matter of fact, Rachel is healed now and will be returning to you soon. I did that until I can talk to the three of you about being around forever. Also, the two of them will have magic." She asked her what sort. "Think of something you'd like to have on other than what you're wearing. Not the size or anything, just something you'd like to have."

The dress appeared on her and fit her so well she had to touch it. The soft material made her skin feel lovely, her body nicely trimmed. When she looked down at her feet, there were heavy socks, the kind she liked to wear when she didn't care what she had on. Looking at Don when he laughed, Pfeiffer asked him what was so funny.

"That is exactly what I pictured you in. Something beautiful yet serviceable. You and your sister have excellent tastes when it comes to clothing. Beautiful women need to be in beautiful clothing, I've always thought."

Pfeiffer couldn't remember the last time someone told her she was beautiful. Not even Robert had ever told her that. He would usually put her down for— Stopping that train of thought, she asked what else she needed to know.

"We're going to buy you a home close to where we're living. In fact, there is a house on the property we're looking at that has six bedrooms, as well as a full kitchen. I don't know why, but I'm assuming it was a butler's home. I want you to live there so I can go and see you when I want. If it needs to be remodeled, you won't have to worry about that either." She asked if she was going to work for CJ. "No. Never. I want you to live a life of leisure. I want you to be able to come and go as you please and have your own life. However, like I said, I would like for you to be close to me. I need you like I need air."

"So long as I can have furniture that doesn't feel like I'm sitting on a bail of hay when I'm sitting in here, I'm fine with that." She heard the dogs barking and got up to look outside. "They just showed up an hour ago. I know nothing about them, but they sure are noisy when someone is here."

"They're wolves. Shifters. They were sent here by Melisandre, I think." She asked Don if he thought she might need protection. "Yes. That's something else we need to talk to you about. The reason you need the magic too."

The dogs were going wild, and she stood at the front window to see who they were barking at. Just as she was ready to tell the dogs to come to her, a man got out of a car. The glass shattered in the front window just as CJ took her to the floor.

"Are you hurt?" Pfeiffer just stared at her. "Are you hurt? Tell me before I have to strip you down to figure it out. Pfeiffer, please tell me you're not—"

"I'm all right. What was that?" Don was gone, and she could hear someone screaming. She started to get up, but CJ told her to stay down, that someone else might be out there. Just as she was feeling the pain of being thrown to the floor, a little bitty person stood on her chest and asked her if she was all right. "I think so. I'm a little sore from being pushed out of the way. Are you a faerie?"

"Yes, mistress. I am at that. My name is Matt. I've come to be with you. I only just arrived, so I was unable to warn you because we have no connection, but I told Lady CJ, and she acted quickly." She asked him how they could get a connection. "The usual way, my lady. I just take a wee bit of your blood, and we can talk all the time. I will warn you. I'm not one to empty my head just to hear my teeth clanking together. I will talk to you when I need to or if we're talking, but not all the time."

It didn't startle her at all that there was a faerie on her chest. Nor that he had wings. She was not even that upset that what she thought had happened was that someone had shot at her. And right now, Don was out there doing something...well, she didn't want to think about what he might be doing to the person. The cut-off screams had given her enough terrible thoughts.

While she lay there, she gave her blood to the little man. It really didn't take all that much for him, and she didn't need to take his. She wasn't even sure how that would work, so she didn't bring it up. Getting the okay to sit up, she did feel a little sore, but almost as soon as she felt the pulls to her body, they were gone. CJ was sitting on the floor with her when

Don came back into the house.

"I'm assuming he's gone." Don nodded and smiled at her. "Don't tell me, please. I'm at that overwhelmed part right now, and I can't take much more. How about we go into the kitchen, and I figure out how to get the window fixed?"

"I'll fix it." Pfeiffer didn't ask. She didn't want to know how it was going to be fixed by CJ but offered Don a cup of her homemade tea. Her sister joined them a few minutes later. "I reinforced the window this time. You won't have to worry about standing in front of any of the windows now. All right?"

"Am I really in danger? Because someone wants you?" CJ nodded and told her everything, including the part where she was related to the queen of faeries. "So, because you were given to our parents to be hidden away, some jackass thinks we're going to be all right with you being taken from us. I don't think so. I've raised two girls all the way up into adulthood. No one will mess with me and be able to walk away unscathed."

Both CJ and Don laughed. It was just what they all needed. Pulling down her cookie tin, she laid the cookies on the table while she brewed the tea. There was something so very calming about having to make tea with the leaves. Steeping the tea in hot water and then adding sugar or lemon to it. When she sat the cups in front of the other two and then sat down with her own, she not only felt calmer but less overwhelmed as well.

"This person out there today. I'm assuming he was a human." Don told her that he had been hired, but yes, he'd been human. "What sort of person is coming for you? I don't want to get it wrong here if someone comes calling for you. Will I have to be on the lookout for anything abnormal?"

"I'll give you a little more magic that will help you tell when a person is a human or a shifter. Also, if they have any kind of ill-will in their hearts." The touch was light to her arm, but the magic that CJ gave her seemed to make her head swim just a little. "What do you see when you look at me, Pfeiffer?"

"Wings. Do you have them?" She nodded. "I thought you might. Also, you have a glow around you. White. Like there isn't anything impure in your soul at all. Is that what I'm going to be looking for when I look at someone?"

"Look at Don. Remember, he's not human either." She turned and looked at the big man. She could see him in two different ways. When cocking her head, she could see his beast, the monster side of him. But he didn't look at her like he wanted her hurt. It was as if he was showing himself to her. Letting her see the real vampire. "Do you see him?"

"I do. I can see both of him. Your monster, or whatever you call him, he's right there so I can see him as well. While I understand he can be a killer when necessary, he is showing me that he can also be calm." She looked at CJ. "You do that for him. You calm his inner monster so that he, Don, can control him better, I think."

"That's exactly right, Pfeiffer. She does calm me." When Don put his hand on top of CJ's, the colors for them both changed. The white was gone, this time turning a lovely shade of lavender. They were in love. "Yes to that as well. I am in love with CJ. And she with me. As soon as we can, we're going to get married and live a long and happy life."

She knew they would too. They were made for each other. She was going to have to make some changes in her plans, she thought. Not just for the couple in her kitchen, but for life in general. Pfeiffer wouldn't have to worry about her daughters soon either. There wasn't any way for either of them to leave her. It was selfish, she knew that, but she thought it was perfect. It was, she thought, about time things started to fall into place for her.

"I'll take whatever you give me in the way of support. I'm not stupid enough to think I could do this on my own. However, when I sell our parents' home, I'll make sure you get half of it." Don told her they had plenty of money for several lifetimes. "Then I'll put it away for my lifetimes. And I'm going to have a life now. No more taking life one day at a time, damn it. I'm going to hit it head-on and have some fun."

Don laughed. It was a good laugh and one that she'd bet he didn't share often. Pfeiffer was going to do that as well. Laugh. At herself or something else, but she was no longer going to be sitting back and waiting for things to happen. She was going to make things happen.

Chapter 4

Josh wasn't sure why he'd been arrested last night. They had entered the place he was staying and dragged him out. It had taken him some fast talking to get a nice room, and the police had screwed it up. Josh had been so happy to have been put into a nice bed and a breakfast, despite there being regular coffee with a packet of dried-up creamer. It had been like a taste of heaven to him. Even the shower had put him in a great mood.

However, today while he was sitting here in a jail cell thinking about his plan, he realized he'd have to modify things a little to get what he wanted. Money. That was it, just money so he could live the life he thought he deserved. And Josh did deserve a very full life of leisure. If only Lizzy had married him like she was supposed to.

She had a great deal of money, more than he'd thought she had when he decided that marrying him was her only option. His only one too. After they were wed, he'd planned on keeping her around for a little while, then hiring someone to kill her off. This was after he got himself set up well. Then she'd disappeared. For over a year, she'd been gone, and he'd tried to collect on the insurance policies he'd already taken out on her. Using her money to pay for them was a little funny to him. Fat lot of good it had done him. She'd been contacting her attorney all along, and they wouldn't pay him. Her being alive had fucked him up royally, he thought.

His lunch was coming—he could smell it. Josh hadn't had much to say about his food given to him last night, but today he wanted something nice. Something they'd get from a restaurant, not whatever the cook dreamed up with leftovers. Leaning back on his bed with his hands where they could be seen, his lunch tray was sent into his cell. Getting up, he was dismayed to find that no one had taken his needs seriously when he told him what he'd wanted.

"Hey? I thought that I ordered a steak sandwich with cheese and French fries. Also, this isn't wine." The man delivering his food told him it hadn't been on the menu he'd ordered from last night. "Sure it was. I wrote it on there when the things that were there didn't appeal to me. Can I get a better meal? I mean, come on. This isn't going to cut it with me."

"Isn't that just too bad for you? Eat it or don't. I don't care. But that is the meal you're getting since you thought that writing in what you wanted was going to get you anywhere. This is a jail, not a five-star hotel." The man walked away, then returned. "Are you eating it or not? Like I said, no sweat off my balls if you don't."

"I'll eat it, but I'm doing it under protest." He opened the lid and found a bologna sandwich like the one he'd had last night, a bag of chips, as well as a dish of pudding of some kind. It was green already, so he wasn't touching that shit. "You guys are going to kill me with this. I hope you know that."

The man only walked away. He'd bet that no one called Lizzy for him either. It was entirely her fault he was in here. While he didn't know what he'd done to get here, he was sure she'd done it.

Josh had been set up nicely by telling Lizzy she needed to marry him. Then she'd sat him down, telling him that in order for her to marry him, he had to have a job. Full time. He had asked her about him getting some of her money so he'd not have to find a job, and she told him in no uncertain terms that not only was he not going to get into her money, but she wasn't going to put him on any of her accounts. Lizzy told him he'd have to sign a prenup as well, stating that he got nothing he didn't bring into the marriage. It seemed to him at the time it was going all in her favor and told her that.

"I'm not stupid, Josh. I've worked very hard for what I have. And I'm not going to hand it over to you just because you're thinking that marrying me is a way for you to be rich. I'm rich. You're not. Not unless you have money stashed away somewhere, and you can use that." He'd told her not to be ridiculous. If he had money stashed away, he'd not have to marry her. "The invitations won't go out until you have a good job and are working hard at keeping it."

Not only had she not sent them out, but she'd not even ordered them. She wasn't a very nice person, he found out. But she had money, and he could put up with her rudeness until she was murdered.

"Mr. Hinkley, Mrs. Remy said to tell you she has better things to do than to come here and listen to you complain. You've made your bed. Now you're going to have to take care of yourself." He asked if she was coming to see him. "No. I just told you that. She's not coming here. None of them are. You have a court hearing in the morning. We'll run you to the—"

"What for?" He asked him what he was talking about. "Why do I have a court hearing? I don't even know why I was arrested. Not to mention, you've treated me badly here, so I think that should be punishment enough. Don't you?"

"No. You're a vagrant. You don't have a place to live. No money on you. You don't have a job or even anything in your name except the clothing on your back. Vagrancy is against the law in this town." He said that was why he needed to talk to Lizzy. "She's not coming. What do you expect her to do? Set you up for life while she's living her own?"

"Yes. She owes me that for making rules about us getting married. I know she has money, but she wanted me to get a job. How stupid is that?" The guard said he thought it was very smart of her. "You'd not think that if you were me. I've been looking to marry her for a while, and now she's gone and made it so I got nothing. Now I've been arrested for not having the things she should have been providing for me."

This officer walked away too. It seemed to him that no one else had thought of his brilliant plan. Perhaps they'd thought of it but weren't as savvy as he was about making it work. He'd been so close to sealing the deal that he could have tasted it. Then, like a fart in the window, he was out of everything. Money. Fame. He knew that with money came fame, so he'd been deprived of that as well.

Eating his sandwich, he thought of the things he'd planned for his money. There was a great deal of her money that he wanted, and the things he had been planning for it were huge. A boat. Houses all over the world that he could just go to. She'd have to get him a private jet too. One that was ready at a moment's notice so he could go and come as he pleased.

Someone clearing their throat had him looking up from his nasty meal. "Who are you? And how did you get in here? Do you have a key?" The man said nothing but did stare at him hard. "Look at what they feed you here. Sandwiches with a bag of chips. I wanted a nice steak sandwich, but this is what I got. Why are you in here?"

"My name is Fergus. I'm Lizzy's father. I want you to leave her alone. You're going to end up on the wrong side of me if you don't stop calling her and telling people what a terrible person she is for not marrying you. You're a deadbeat and should have been put down long ago." Josh told him Lizzy didn't have a father. The man only cocked his brow at him. "How the hell do you think she came to be if she didn't have a father? You really are a moron, aren't you?"

"No. I'm not. I'm very smart. I need you to tell her to leave her current husband so I can have what I want." Josh's head exploded in pain, so much, so he felt blood coming from his nose. "What the fuck was that? Christ, that felt like a jackhammer hit me in the head."

"I did that. I'll do more to you if you don't fucking leave my daughter alone." When he opened his mouth, Josh saw the fangs. He didn't believe this man was a vampire any more than he was. Laughing, he told him that was a good try, but he wasn't buying it. "You're not buying the fact that I just showed you what I am? Lizzy is a vampire, too just so you know. So is her husband. The one she's not leaving. Especially not for someone like you."

"What's wrong with me?" The man listed off all the things he thought Josh was afflicted with. "You see, those are all my good traits. I'm lazy, yes. But why should I have to work when there is someone out there with more money than they can spend? I can do that. You said I was a drain on society. No, I don't get any federal assistance. It's a stupid rule again. I have to have worked someplace in order for them to give me money to live. And people call me a moron. If I had a job, which I'm not going to get, why would I need assistance? See? People like me need to be in charge of shit like this. Not that I'd stoop so low as to work for them, but hell, it's all fucked up."

"You seriously believe it's all right not to have an income? A place to live or anything like that?" Josh told him that was right. It was his right to do that. "At the expense of anyone you can con into marrying you or just giving money to you?"

"Yes. Like you, for example. You have money, right?" He told him he had a great deal of it. "Why don't you give a lot of it to me, and I'll go away? At least for a little while. I mean, I have needs too. And wants. You give me, say, seven-million dollars, and

I'll move out of town. Then for the rest of my life, you can make sure I have at least a million a month to live on, and I won't bother your daughter. See that right there? I didn't have to work on that plan. It just popped into my head. I'm really good at planning shit like that."

"I have a better plan. Why don't I just kill you right now and be done with it? No one would be the wiser. They'd just think you thought things through and decided you'd kill yourself. That's the best route, I think. At least over me sending you money each month." He told him that didn't work for him. "What if I were to tell you I don't give a good flying fuck what works for you? I want you out of her life, and now out of mine, and my solution solves it all."

"But I'd be dead. Doesn't that bother you at all? For a man such as myself to be dead? Think of all the things that could be missed out on if I were to end up like you want." He asked him what things. "Like me living the life I want. I know what you're thinking. That it's all about me. Well, it is all about me. Me getting what I want and believe I need. I'm not saying I really need that much money each month, but what if I did? Then I'd have to come back here and make sure you're going to give me more money. It's just too time-consuming. Just give me the money now and then monthly without making me have to bother you about it. That, if you haven't guessed, is too much like work. And I don't want to work. That's the entire point of this."

Fergus stood up and looked down at him. Josh had never been one to be self-conscious about people's opinions of him. So letting the man look at him all he wanted, he looked the man over too.

He was big. He'd give him that. Not a bit of fat on him either. His hair was full and long, curly too. Probably one of those romance cover models. He'd heard that was a good way to make money, but he didn't have any desire to exercise all the time to look that good. When the man touched his hand to his forehead, Josh smiled up at him.

"You call my daughter again, mention her name about it being her fault you're in the mess you're in, and I'll come back here and rip out your throat. I'm not going to pussyfoot around about it either. I will show up when you least expect it and kill you." Josh told him that wasn't very nice. "Nice or not, that's what is going to happen to you if you fuck around and bother her again."

Then he was gone. Josh went to the mirror over his commode and saw that he had blood on his face. Washing up, he noticed his neck was bleeding as well. When he tried to examine it in the cheap mirror, it looked like two puncture marks. The man had really done his job well, Josh thought. Making it look like he'd been bitten. He sat back down with his washcloth over the wound because it hadn't stopped bleeding yet. Laughing out loud, he thought he'd have to remember this. Tell a woman he was a vampire and then put two marks on her skin. He wouldn't bite anyone, that was just gross, but the thought of someone thinking he was a cool vamp had its merits. Yes, he was going to do that the next time he got around someone he was going to get money from.

When dinner came around, he didn't feel well. Even sitting up was sort of making him sick. He just knew something he'd had for lunch had made him sick. Blaming it on the food got him yelled at again, but he was just too tired to argue with anyone. It was a bit like work if you asked him.

Going back to sleep, he felt someone move him at one point, but he was too exhausted to give too much thought to it. When he woke up again, he realized he was in the hospital. Josh didn't even care enough to ask them why he was there. He thought someone had tried to poison him. He was going to sue them all. Then he'd have some fucking cash.

~*~

Don and CJ owned a home. The paperwork had been signed not an hour ago, and now they were going through it with the faeries sent to help them get it ready to move into. He was enjoying having them around, but he wanted CJ all to himself more than he wanted a nicely decorated house.

"Sir, you're not paying attention again." He'd been doing that all morning, drifting off on some thought that had something to do with CJ being naked and him inside her. The faerie, Cody, had been trying to keep him centered since they had arrived. "I believe the mistress is beginning to make decisions with the house on her own." He asked him where she was. "Three rooms down. She's been in there for some time now."

"Look. I need to spend some alone time with CJ. I mean, we need to bond." Cody told him that would be a good thing. "Then pardon me for being rude, but you need to leave. Now. And take the other faeries with you. I promise you, I'll pay more attention after today."

"Yes, my lord." He could tell that Cody was struggling not to laugh. Don turned away when the need to laugh too caught him off guard. "I'll make sure you're not disturbed for...I was going to say until tomorrow, but you call out to me if you're in need of something else. I'll take care that the bedroom is romantic for the two of you."

When he left him, Don wondered which room the master bedroom was. He'd missed it someplace along the line and hated that. However, watching Cody and the three faeries that had been with them all morning enter one of the rooms, he made a note of it. Don did wonder if romantic for a faerie was the same as romantic for a human or shifter. He'd find out, he supposed.

Finding CJ didn't prove as easy as he'd thought it would be. It occurred to him as he opened all the doors that there were a lot of bedrooms in this house. Someone might have told him at one point, but his mind wasn't centering well. When he found her in the bathroom at the end of the hall, she looked like she was thinking hard on something. Don asked her if he could help her.

"This room looks off. Like it's not right." He didn't know what she meant, so he tried to figure it out as she went on to explain. "The walls are too close. Like the wall with the shower in it is out of proportion to what you'd think. Am I making sense?"

"I get it now. Let me look on the other side of this." He went into the hall and then back in the room with her. "You're right. It's like there should be about five or so more square feet than is showing. You think there is something behind this wall?"

"I don't know. But even if it's only blank space, it would be nice to have this room enlarged, don't you think? I mean, it's not really crowded, but it would be nice for the extra room." He knocked on the wall, listening to see if he could figure out something. Calling out for Cody, he figured that if anyone could get to the other side, it would be a faerie. CJ asked the little man if he could figure it out for them. "I just want to know what is behind here. Please don't tell me if there are dead bodies piled up. We just bought this house, and I don't want a crime scene here."

Cody nodded and disappeared. When he returned, he looked at him first, then at CJ. They were both a little nervous when it took him so long to get around to answering them. Cody looked back at him.

"I don't know what it is. You could see, can you not? Go into the room beyond here?" He'd honestly never thought of doing it himself. So willing himself to the other room, he looked around for several minutes before he figured it out. Laughing hard, he went to where CJ and Cody were. "It's nothing I'm familiar with, my lord. I am sorry."

"It's fine, Cody. It took me a few seconds as well to—"

"If you two are done, I'd like to know what the fuck it is. What the hell is on the other side that you had to laugh about?" Instead of telling her, he wrapped her into his arms and took her. "Oh, Don. It's beautiful."

It was too. Even as dirty as it was, cobwebs hanging from everything, it was lovely. He wondered why anyone would have done such a thing to such a wonderful space. The windows were from floor to ceiling and boarded up from the outside. They went all the way around the space to provide light for the plants that had been left behind to die. There was a mural on the ceiling, as well as stone on the floor that he bet was beautiful too. He could just imagine someone taking a long soak in a tub and being able to see the windows filled with plants.

"I want this opened up." He said he did as well. When she put her fingers into one of the long-dead plants' containers, the plant began to green up. The leaves appeared and unfurled so that the entire plant, a fig tree, came back to life within seconds. She touched the other plants as well. "Will you mind if I have the faeries fix this up for us? I so want to be able to look into this room and see all of this. It's nothing I would have imagined it would be, and I love it."

Cody joined them in the room a few seconds after CJ called for him. The little man, knowing what his mistress wanted, was vibrating with excitement to do this for them. The windows were uncovered first. The room flooded with light.

"Once we have this cleaned up, my lady, it will be simply the most beautiful bathing room in the world. I think I should like to have myself a little space in here as well. I would love that." She told him he could so long as she wasn't bathing at the time. "Oh no. I'd not do that to either of you. No. Just when I have a few minutes, it would restore me in the colder months when it is difficult for us to be warm. This will be wonderful, my lady. Yes, I can almost see it now."

They left him to his work. Others joined him,

and Don could hear him telling them what was to be done. Don did wonder if the ceiling was glass too, but there was so much filth on the rooftop that he'd just have to wait and find out. Taking CJ's hand into his, he led her down to what he hoped was the master bedroom.

Cody had outdone himself. The room was, simply put, a master suite made for a queen. The four-post bed had a lacy canopy on the top. The furniture in the room was oak. It looked warm and inviting like you could run your hands over the surface all day and never get a splinter. There were no curtains on the two windows on either side of the bed, but there were black-out shades for him to pull when he needed to rest.

There was also a bucket of ice with a bottle of champagne chilling in it. A box of chocolates that were as dark and rich looking as any he'd ever seen before. The bathroom wasn't nearly as nice as the one down the hall, but he decided that if after it was cleaned up, they both still loved it, he'd have the faeries make the same for their bathroom. Only larger and roomier.

"This is very nice. If you're trying to seduce me, you didn't have to go to so much effort. I want you as badly as you do me." He told her that Cody had done it, but he was going to romance her as much as he could from now on. "All right. I don't think anyone has ever done this much for me. Even if you didn't do it, it's still very nice."

Pulling out the bottle, he opened it up and poured the two of them some of the sparkling wine. Sipping it, all he could think about was that he was going to make love to his mate. That the two of them were going to be joined in a way that would bind them like nothing that humans ever did with their loved ones.

"I wanted to tell you how very much I love you, CJ. From the bottom of my feet to my head. My heart only belongs to you." She wrapped her arms around his waist. CJ told him that she loved him too. "I want to make love to you. Take you over and over until neither of us can move."

"Good. I'm glad you're finally getting around to it. I've been trying to figure out a way to give my poor body some relief for days now." He laughed. She was so incredibly honest he couldn't help but love her. "I'm going to change into something pretty. So when I show you this, you're not to pounce on me. I want you to admire what I've been thinking about for you. You can be naked. In fact. I'd love it if you were just standing there with a smile and a hard cock. I'm going to suck you dry."

He couldn't swallow. Don was also sure that his head had lost about fifty percent of his thought process. When she stepped into the bathroom, he was still standing there when she came out. The nighty, the flimsy thing she had on, didn't hide anything from his view. Don felt like he was in a candy store and told that he could only have one treat. But he also knew she was all his.

"You're not naked." She laughed when he made everything he had on disappear. "What do you think of my itty bitty tiny little nighty, Don? Isn't it just about the sexiest thing you've seen?"

Words wouldn't pass his lips. The moment she turned around, showing him the back of the thing, he knew on some level that he was going to be in serious trouble here. If he didn't come right now, he'd be lucky if he made it to the bed in one piece. As soon as she dropped down in front of him, taking his cock into her mouth, Don held tightly to the oak post on the bed and prayed he didn't break it.

"Holy Christ, yes."

All she'd done was lick the crown of his cock, and he came. It was a short hard punch to his system that left him staggering for more. Or less. His body wasn't sure what he wanted right now. But when she took him to her mouth, swallowing, so he was past the tight muscles in the back of her throat, Don started fucking her. He truly knew he was going to die and didn't care.

Don lost all sense of time and his surroundings. If there had been someone in the room with them, wanting to kill them both, he would not have had the brain cells to do anything about it. Looking down at CJ to tell her he was dying, he saw her look up at him. He'd never experienced anything like looking into her eyes right at that moment.

"Your eyes. They're beautiful." When she blinked, he nearly forgot she had his cock in her mouth. "They're like a solar system. Blues with sparking stars. Reds and golds too. And it's moving. Christ, it's moving like the clouds in the sky."

She stood up then, her face wet with his cum. Lying on the bed now, he could only stare at her. Not only were her eyes different, but while lying on the bed, her wings spread out behind her, the colors so magnificent he was sure there were no names for the lot of them.

"Do you want a child with me?" He nodded, thinking that a daughter by her would be just as beautiful. "I'm fertile, Don. If you want a child with me right now, then take me. We'll have created a child so powerful she'll surpass even the queen."

While he did hear what she was saying, none of it mattered to him. A child. Her belly swollen with his babe. Getting onto the bed with her, he kissed her while touching as much of her body as he could. Nipping at her skin, he tasted her rich blood, spiked not only with her lust but also the magic she had. Drinking from her in small sips was making his head swim, his body float. When he entered her, Don felt his beast roar out with his pleasure.

Her cry of pleasure was more than he could have hoped for. She came three times even before he moved. Her hands wrapping around his shoulders gave him her throat. As soon as he licked the pounding pulse there, he heard her cry out with her need to be bitten, as strong as his need to bite. Sinking his teeth into her throat, Don came.

It was profound. Magical. Every Christmas and birthday he'd ever had. His body bowed back, his mouth still at her throat when he came a second time. Taking her harder hurt him, his body nearly spent as it was. But when she dug her nails into his back, rising up, literally up and off the bed, he emptied himself into her once again before he dropped over her as they floated to the bed.

He knew he was heavy. That he needed to roll off her. But there was nothing left of him. Not even the strength to make her more comfortable. Closing his eyes, telling himself he'd only rest for a moment, Don knew he'd be lucky if he ever rose again. She had quite nicely killed him with sex.

Chapter 5

CJ wasn't as much worried about Don as she was missing him. He'd been sleeping, resting, Bancroft told her, for three days now. Checking on him again, he was still in the same position he'd been when she'd left him the morning after they'd made love.

"He's resting, CJ. There is very little that can be done to wake him. I'd say it's also the magic you told me you received that day. He's an old vamp, so he maybe has to blend what he has with what you've given him." That made sense, but she didn't like it any better. "I promise you. He will wake and be rested up enough to chase you around the house again."

She hoped so. But she wasn't getting anything done, making sure he was all right. Going back down to her office, she was glad to see everything was up and running. The computer she'd ordered was perfect. She'd have to thank Kelly for hooking her up with someone that could get her into a secure network. After that, she'd been able to tweak things, so she was about as safe as she'd ever been when using her computer.

Picking up the phone, she called Bancroft. "There are currently five nests you had me find for you. One of them is just about ten miles from where you currently are." She gave him the address. "It looks like there are ten people in the lower levels of the house. I can't tell if they're human or not, but their heat signatures are nearly blue."

"Tell me again what that means. Before I forget to tell you, there are people in town looking for your sister. No one is giving them any information, but I wanted to give you a heads up." CJ thanked him. "It's my pleasure. Now, what does them being blue mean again?"

"They're cold. As in, I'm thinking they're human, but they're being drained slowly by the vampires." He asked her if there might be more that had already died. "Good possibility. I can check on that without you going there if you want."

"You can? Great. I'd like to know what I might meet up with first. If you can do that, you'll save me a bit of time and bloodshed."

She went to the window in her office and

reached out beyond where she was. She didn't need to have the window open to do that, but she got a better connection with earth when there was nothing separating her from it. CJ could have reached the other nests, too, to see how many people were around them, but she didn't want to overwhelm him. Bancroft seemed really stressed out lately. Going back to the phone when she had his information, she knew he wasn't going to be happy with what she had to tell him.

"There are four still alive as of a few seconds ago. The signatures have faded out to nothing, so the others are presumed dead. The vampires are having themselves a nice party with the remaining four, and they'll be dead before anyone can save them. You should also know that the vamps are not very old. I'd say less than a year, all five of them. Aren't they supposed to report to you or something?" He told her they were supposed to be, but he'd not been notified. "You'll have to teach me how to tell how old they are, as I'm only guessing about their age by how they're acting like idiots. I'd think older vampires would be a stick in the mud like you are. Also, I'm not sure this is important or not, but four of them were turned by the same vampire. I don't know who the original baby vamp maker is, but I'm thinking he's dead. His child turned the others."

"So this guy gets turned, and then he turns a

bunch more to be with him. That is grounds for death. I wonder if he's aware of it." She closed her eyes, concentrating on the single maker. She told Bancroft he felt he was above such laws. "Is he one of those vampires that think all humans are just cattle?"

"No, he's just a dickhead that wants to be able to kill indiscriminately, and there is no one stronger than him. At least as far as he thinks. He did kill his maker when he brought him to task about making more vampires. This kid—because that's all he is at eighteen—is really getting on my last nerve. He's just killed one of his babies. They're dancing on his body. Why don't you let me take care of them for you? In fact, it would make my day."

"How?" She asked him if he really wanted to know. "When you put it like that, no, I guess I don't. However, I'd have to be there, or you could face charges for taking them out. I'm not sure why that rule is in there. I'll have to work on taking it out. The issue being that if I remove a rule, I have to replace it with another one. Dumbest thing I've ever heard of. Anyway, when do you want to meet there?"

"I'm not busy right now." He laughed and said he'd meet her there. "All right. Don't be alarmed when you see the warrior faeries with me. I don't know if you were told this or not, but they're mine to call upon while I'm in this realm."

"I didn't know that, but it's good to know. Are

faeries afraid of vampires? I don't know why, but I think that was something I heard once." She said these weren't. "I wonder where that came from then."

"More than likely because of the rule you're going to remove. They were never allowed to kill your kind when necessary because of that law. Faeries don't kill just for the sport of it, but your kind has been known to kill them. If you can take that rule out, I will promise you that they'll come to you too when you have a nest problem." He thanked her again. "No problem. I'll see you there in a few minutes."

Calling to her army, she knew that once they were at the nest, all of them would be armed with not just magic but also armor. These faeries were not ones to fuck with. When they were told to kill, they did it with the fastest and most deadly way they knew, usually going for the heart and out the other side of a body.

She was standing there waiting on Bancroft when Don finally contacted her. CJ nearly fell to her knees. The relief of hearing from him was so profoundly wonderful. When he asked where she was, she told him and then asked if he'd join them. He was there before she could give him the address. He told her he'd followed her scent.

Bancroft called to the vampires. They had no choice but to come to him. He wasn't one to mess with either. When the four of them came out of the house, she shook her head. They hadn't even bothered cleaning themselves up before meeting their king. Not only were they covered in blood, but they were covered in the ash of their fellow vamp they'd killed. She knew just who the leader was as soon as he bowed to them and smiled.

"Oh, lordship of the vampires. What is it we can do for you today? Or did you bring us a tasty treat? She looks fine." Both Bancroft and Don growled. Even the hair on her arms stood up. But dumbass seemed to either be dumber than she thought, or he had no idea what the fuck he was up against. "What? You don't think we know a fine piece of ass when we see it?"

The others were laughing now. Since their leader seemed to be doing all right, they figured they could as well. One of his babies came to stand in front of her. Smiling at him, she suggested he back up.

"What do you say you and I have us a little fun?" Putting her hand on Don's chest, she told him she had this. "Yeah, big boy. Go away and let the adults play."

When the vamp touched her, putting only his finger on her cheek, he was dead even before he realized she'd killed him. All it took for her to end his life was to say back off once more, then she took her sword and removed first his hand, then his head. He was ash when she looked at the others.

"Woo, that isn't right." She took a step toward the others as the ringleader kept telling her she wasn't playing fair. Bancroft was also telling them the laws they'd broken, as well as the penalties they were facing. "We don't need no stinking laws."

He turned to the others and laughed. They were no longer joining in on his fun. It was obvious to all of them that they were beginning to realize they'd fucked up. As soon as the dumbass turned to her again, Bancroft told them they were going to die.

"Any last requests?" He only laughed at her when she made it clear they were going to die. "Do you have a family? Someone we can tell that you're no longer around? Ah, so you killed them as well. Well, it's been real. Warriors. Kill them."

She turned her back to the carnage. There would be little to nothing left of them when the warriors killed them. A bit of cloth here, some toenails or fingernails as well. Bancroft looked at her when she told him it was finished. Also, that her army would take care that their deaths would be filed away as natural causes.

"In a few hours, someone will find the bodies of the ones in the lair here. It will look like a bad accident, and their deaths will be blamed on the heating element going out or something like that, and nothing more." She grinned at him when he cocked a brow at her. "Or if you have a better idea, we can do this your way."

"Remind me never to get on your bad side." She said he'd not so long as he allowed her to help him on occasion. "All right. Why? I mean, it was over so quickly, it's doubtful there was any kind of joy for anyone."

"It wasn't joy they were seeking, my lord, but the opportunity to do something for the vampire king." Lola sat on her shoulder as she spoke to Bancroft. "These men have caused us great harm as well in what they've done here. The earth in this spot is dead because they had to be killed. The house that sits there, it is no longer a place we'll go to when we need to hide from the weather or humans. It is spoiled. But if you would allow us to, we'll enrich the ground, remove the house, and let the earth begin again. If you would so wish it."

"I do. And thank you. Your mistress here, she said you'd help me, and you did. Thank you all. I will be happy to furnish you with treats, as well as other things for your help here today." Lola thanked him before flying away. Bancroft asked CJ if that was all they needed. "Yes. For now. But if you'd allow them free reign with this sort of trouble, they'll clear out a nest before they cause damage to the town they're in."

"I can do that. So long as they report to me before they do it." CJ said she'd make sure he had plenty of warning. "Thank you for this, CJ. You have saved me a great deal of trouble by helping today. I owe you."

"You can repay me by making Don your second." They both looked at her. "You need someone. And I'm thinking with what he has and what I've given him, there is no one better to protect the king of vamps. Besides, as it stands right now, you're going to need more protection when your children are born."

"We've not told anyone that they're twins." She said she was one with the earth and knew shit like that. "Christ, you make me laugh so much. Yes, I'll take Don as my second if he will do it."

"I will be honored, Banny." They shook hands on it, and Bancroft disappeared. Don took her into his arms and held her. "You're very sneaky when you want to be, aren't you?"

"I can be. How rested are you? I mean, I've been waiting for you to wake for the last three days so that we could have some more fun." He asked her if she was kidding that he'd really been down for three days. "No. Bancroft said you must have needed it for the magic. Now that I see you up and around, I think he was right. You were out so that your body could get used to the magic."

"While I haven't any idea to dispute your word on that, I have to admit that I do feel a great deal better than I have in a while." Don kissed her on the top of her head and then pulled her back enough to look at her. "Your eyes, they still look like a solar system. Is that because we've bonded, or something else?"

"I don't have to hide anymore. I can let more of me show at a time, and no one will be surprised by it. Little things like my eyes, they'll see it, but not mention it as they might think they missed it before." She grinned at him. "Do you think anyone will notice if I suddenly start walking around with these big fucking wings dragging behind me?"

"I don't know. I mean, it seems to me that when you're around, people only notice how simply beautiful in your heart that you are." She told him he was being sappy. "Perhaps. But I love you anyway, so that's all right. I have about fifty things I could do to you today, but since I've been out of it for so long, there are things I have to check on."

"Me as well. I was waiting on you to get up and didn't get shit done. Now that I know you're all right, I feel like I can get away from you for a little while." They both laughed after looking wounded. "You know what I mean. I'll see you later?"

"Yes. I'll contact you when I need you. Don't forget there are the house things we need to pick up as well." She told him what she'd done out of boredom. "Good. I love that you ordered everything online. There is one thing I've never been fond of doing, and that's shopping. Thank you for that."

As they parted ways, she was contacted by Bancroft again. *I give you and your team full authority to take care of the other nests in the area. I will talk to other leaders of kisses around the world and see how they want to handle the issues they might have going on.* She said she could do that. *I only need you to give me the same information every time you go out. Where it is when you took care of it, and if you can, the names of the vampires. Also,* Kelly said with that information, she can make sure any bodies on the premises are found.

I like that. Teamwork. However, I will let you know that sometimes it might only be a single vampire that needs to be taken out, and we might not have time to notify you. He told her so long as she could justify it, he was fine with her taking care of it. *Thank you. I guess you're not as much of a stick in the mud as I first thought.*

Gee, thanks. He laughed. *I just spoke to Don. He and I have to form a bond as well. Just a blood-letting thing. If you'd be there, along with Kelly, I'd appreciate it. It's formality doing this, but I'd like to go by the rules as much as I can.*

After telling him she'd be there with Don whenever he said, they closed the connection. Sending Lola on her way to take care of the other nests, she made her way to the hospital. There were things there she still needed to take care of as well.

She entered the hospital and went to the third floor. Cody had told her a man had died that morning of what appeared to be a bloodletting. CJ was asked to go and check it out and not to let Bancroft know. The only reason she did it was so he could be ruled out as the one that had killed the young man. Bloodletting was a serious way to get your ass in trouble with Mother Earth. As soon as she entered the morgue without anyone seeing her, she had a good idea what had happened. It was none of the vampires at the house, but she had a good idea who had killed Josh Hinkley.

~*~

Don's first duty to Banny was to find the killer of a human that had been in the jail locally. He already knew who had killed the young human. He also knew now why he'd been in jail. According to the information he'd gotten from Banny, as well as from Lizzy that morning, he had a good handle on a lot of reasons that someone might well have wanted the man dead. He was, in a word, a dick.

"Why are you here?" He smiled at CJ and told her where he'd been told to start. "Well, that's just stupid. I told you where the man was, and coming here is a waste of your time. Did he even listen to me when I gave him the information? I swear to you, one minute I like the man, then for the next two or three days, I want to string him up by his balls. Why aren't you where I told you the man—?"

To stop CJ from ranting more, he pulled her tightly into his arms and kissed her. The morgue wasn't the most romantic of places, but he had to come here for the soul reason that he'd been told to. Telling CJ that had her ranting against his palm over her mouth.

"We must do this by the books." She asked him why that mattered. "Because the man is in the public, and killing him outright will cause a lot of trouble for a great many people. What do you think will happen when they first find out he's disappeared? Then secondly, that he's a vampire? I'm betting no one he works with is aware of that. And if they are, they're going to hide him away if we say a word about him doing this. It'll be justified in their minds."

"Oh." He let her go. "I guess you're right, but I don't have to like it. He murdered the man for no other reason than he was annoying. Everyone is annoying to me. What if I went around killing off people when they annoyed me? There wouldn't be anyone left. That's what would happen."

"I'm so very happy you restrain yourself." He watched her face to see if she could tell he was joking with her. Sometimes when she was intense about something, she wouldn't get it. "Are you going to keep following me around, or do you have something else you can do? If you can't decide, I'd like for you to find something else to do. I'm sort of excited to be doing this for Bancroft."

"I know you are. And I know you won't get hurt. But this guy, he's killed once. I'm worried he's going to have done it be —" She stopped talking and moved him back against the wall. When the door beside them opened up, he pulled shadows around them both.

"I tell you, I saw her go in here. She's like trying to catch a fart in the wind." The man speaking looked around, then back at the person who'd not come through the open door yet. "She's not in here. I don't know why you're so worried about her. We don't have any way of keeping her from finding out she's been tagged to be killed by you."

Don didn't move when the man's companion came into the room. Not a person as he'd thought, but Cody, CJ's faerie. CJ looked up at him when Cody went to sit on the shoulder of the first man.

"I have to tell you, I've enjoyed giving her false hope that no one will find her. Also, you do know that if she goes to the queen, it's going to be all over for us. She'll get the magic she has coming to her, and we'll be out of luck in doing much more than just taking her." The man asked Cody what he meant as he opened and closed the drawers the bodies were cooled in. "She'll get all this special power. I thought for sure we had the wrong person when she never seemed to use anything but just mundane magic. But then she met her mate, and it was like she'd been pulled from darkness, and there it was for me to see. I cannot wait for her to be gone from my life. I like her, don't get me wrong, but she's nothing compared to the queen."

"You're sure you have the right woman, right?" Cody said he was ninety-nine percent sure of it. "Yeah, well, it's the one percent that worries me. What if, by that small margin, she's the wrong chick? Do you think the queen will give us what we want because we have this person she's related to? Then she finds out it really isn't? That worries me more than anything. Then there is what my boss will say."

"I've yet to meet him. Is he as badass as everyone says?" The man said it was a woman he worked for. "A woman? Well, I guess they are as smart as men when it comes to planning things. I just want to get this over with and move on. I've found me a person I can live with, and she and I are going to go all the way across these states and never return. Not that I could, but you never know what sort of fun I can get into elsewhere."

"She's not so bad, I guess. I mean, I've worked for a— Here he is."

The drawer was opened all the way, and Don could smell the vampire on the body. Asking CJ if it was the man from the jail, she didn't take her eyes off the two in the room with them. Shaking her a little, she turned to him, and he could see the tears in her eyes.

To be betrayed was one thing. But to be deceived by someone you thought of as your friend was something else altogether. Cody and CJ had been together for a long time, he thought, and to find out now it had been a setup from the beginning would have hurt him as well. He held her tighter when the man picked up the body and put it over his shoulder to leave.

"I'll just have to dispose of this body, then I can work on the things I've been assigned for CJ. Why do you think taking her mate is going to do anything to her? I mean, from what I've heard all her life, she's nothing but a hardass that needs to be put down." When she started to move toward to the two men, he had to hold her tightly. Telling her they'd plan something for them had her calming down. "I think she has a nice body, but nothing more than that. I'd have to make sure to tape her mouth up when I fucked her so she'd not be bitching the entire time."

Taping up your mouth would take away the greatest pleasure I've ever known. She was hurt, and he knew it. Cuddling her into his arms, he explained to her what he was going to do to the other man as soon as he caught up with him. *So you see, it's a good thing you came here to ask me a question. We might not have known to what extent things are for the two of them.*

Cody is going to die. The other man as well, but Cody is mine to kill. Don said he would allow her to face him if she promised to wait for him to take care of the other things first. *I need you to be caught by them.*

Why? She explained to him the plan that was working in her head. *I see. I get kidnapped so you can show them what a real bad person you are.* She told him she was a badass. *Yes. Well, pardon me for that. But I know your ass intimately, and there is not a thing wrong with it as far as I can see.*

The two of them watched the men, following them out of the hospital and to a van he took down the license plate for. He didn't care that they stole the body he'd been there to look at, but it did bother him that CJ was so hurt. Don reached out to Bancroft to let him know what was going on. He, too, was hurt that Cody was in on this scam.

Are you with them now? Don told him they were following them to see where this led. *You let me know, and I'll be there to help. I know CJ has her army, but this is personal now. I want them to suffer, and I'm sure she won't do that. To think that – We'll have to tell Melisandre too. She's not going to be very happy.*

Not yet. Bancroft asked him why not. *I don't know yet, but I did just have a thought that she might be the big boss ordering things around. While I'm not sure that is possible – she did give us the magic that would make us immortal, but I don't know for sure that she even did that. It bears a little thought. Don't you think?*

Christ, I hope you're wrong. He said he did as well. *All right. Then who do you think we should notify? I'm not going to be in hot water over not informing someone of what we think is happening. Anyone.*

Aurora. She is the queen of just about everything to do with the earth, correct? That seemed to satisfy both of them. *She's been around for a long time, so far as we know. Not to mention there doesn't seem to be any connection between her and CJ. I don't know that I trust anyone at this moment, but like you said, we have to do something.*

In the end, Bancroft was going to contact Aurora. Neither of them knew the woman—just who she was really. She'd been around, they knew, for a very long time. But since they'd never had a reason to contact her, he supposed they'd not gotten on her radar. Yet, anyway.

Don and CJ followed the men to a place in the middle of a great field. Once there, the body was removed, then put into the house. CJ stayed with the two of them while Don made his way to the large open area that smelled of death.

Bancroft. I need you to come to me now. And if you have contacted Aurora, it might be a great idea to have her come along with you. He asked him what he'd found. *It might be better if you were to just come to me. This is bad. Really bad.*

Aurora appeared first. Then Bancroft. They all stood there, looking into a manmade cavern filled with bodies. Not just of humans, though there were a lot of those, but faeries as well. Don wasn't sure what was going on, but he had a feeling the shit was just about to hit the fan, and he was thrilled to death that he wasn't going to be on the receiving end of the wrath that was coming off the two super-beings standing beside him.

Don, they're on their way out of the house with the body. They've cut out his heart for some reason. He might not have known before this meeting, but he had a feeling he could guess now. It would be proof that not only was the man dead but also that they'd killed him. *I'm not sure what is going on.*

Come out here, love. I'm thinking we're about to get a lesson in superpower between a king of vampires and the queen of the earth. She asked him if he was drunk. *No. But for the first time in my entire life, I surely wish I was.*

Chapter 6

Melisandre moved through her world to the one where her queen was living. It was nice to be there. No pressure for her to be working all the time. Also, since she'd first been promoted to being the queen of faeries, she'd been enjoying herself with the perks that came with her job. Like being able to go to different parts of the world without any trouble from other beings that would beg her for help. They didn't know her and therefore knew nothing about her position to the queen.

Being summoned this late in the day was concerning, but whatever the queen wanted, she got. Smiling to herself, she sat down on the sofa when she was shown to the room in which she was going to talk to her. A cup of tea appeared in front of her, as well as some lavender cookies, her favorite. Queen Aurora appeared a few seconds after she'd drank her first cup of tea.

"I hope you're well, Melisandre." She said she was and was glad to be invited to her home. "You're very welcome. I have a great many things I want to talk to you about. The tea that you've drank had a potion in it that will require you to tell me the truth. Now. What are you doing with Cody and a man named Benson?"

Melisandre nearly swallowed the bite of cookie she had in her mouth whole. Choking a little, she watched her boss as she sat there without any qualms about letting her cough her head off. She was terrified at that moment, more than she'd ever been.

"While I know Cody and that he belongs to CJ, I'm afraid I don't know who Benson is." Aurora said for her to think hard. She did, too, trying to remember anyone she might have contact with that would go by that name. "I'm very sorry, my queen, but I don't know anyone by that name. If you could let me see his face, that might help."

The man appeared in front of her. The shape his body was in startled her somewhat. He'd been torn up. She'd bet anything that he'd suffered greatly and that his death hadn't been quick. Studying his face hard, she knew whatever her answer was for this question would be a matter of life and death. More importantly, *her* life and death.

"I've seen him before. With Cody. Now that I think on it, I've only seen him a handful of times, but never with anyone but Cody." She looked at Aurora when the body disappeared. "I'm assuming he's done something with Cody or to CJ. I want you to know I had nothing to do with whatever it was."

"I know that now. However, I will tell you there are many clues out there that led right to your doorstep." Melisandre thought about the body she'd seen and the reason she'd been brought here. She asked Aurora if she thought she'd done something wrong. "Not now, no. But I was going to kill you if what I'd been led to believe was true."

Melisandre didn't know what to say to that. Aurora was the only one that could kill her. She didn't even have to justify it to anyone, as she was the only being that everyone answered to. When offered another cup of tea, she declined it. Not because she thought it might be poisoned, but because she'd lost her appetite for anything right now.

"I'm not going to do it." Melisandre thanked her. "No. I must thank you for being honest. I didn't put anything into your drink. You had to know that as well."

"I never thought about it. Honestly, I wasn't even thinking I could be in trouble like this until you mentioned Cody. I have been having some issues with him. Not bad things, but he'd not come to me when it was— I just had a thought. Does CJ know he's been caught at whatever is going on?"

"She killed him."

Nodding, Melisandre shivered. The look of the body came back to her, and she knew that whatever CJ had done to Cody was going to be a thousand times worse. Looking at the queen when she said her name, Melisandre was suddenly sick. It only took a touch from Aurora to make her illness disappear.

"She made his death something that all will think about when they think to go against what I have decreed a law. Keeping the kiss of Bancroft safe is something that has been in place for many decades. Longer, I think, than even you've been alive."

"Thank you." Aurora moved back to her seat across from her. "May I ask who you might think has made this my fault? I'm assuming I wasn't the only one that was supposed to be guilty."

"I haven't any idea at the moment. CJ, she's working on it. I don't think whoever she catches at this will live long. And if they do, they will wish for death with every breath they take." Melisandre had seen CJ at work once. She'd taken on a troll that had—

"You've thought of something."

"The troll overlord. I think his name is River." Aurora said she knew of him. "Several months ago—I don't think it's been quite a year now—he came to me with news about someone polluting his waterways. I did go and see to it but found nothing that hadn't been left behind by his people. But he insisted someone was making sure they could no longer live near the water. I sent CJ there. She…to be honest with you, I believe she only told me it had been taken care of. Nothing more was spoken about it, as I had been working on the fields for the spring. Yes, that's it. Springtime. I was so busy, but I did make sure he had someone looking around."

"Did you ask CJ about it more than her telling you it was taken care of?" She said she'd only just remembered. But she had trusted her judgment on it. "I would have too, to be honest with you. She's never let us down before. All right. I will call her here. I would like you to remain so you can work out with her what happened. But I must ask, what made that thought pop into your head?"

"I don't know. At the time he came to me, he was very angry. He was telling me all kinds of stories about how his mate had been murdered. That the person who had done it had been harassing his people for a long time. Since I know nothing about the trolls, and he told me that none of my faeries did it, I told him he'd have to take care that it was looked into himself." Aurora again agreed with what she'd done. "I never thought to go back and get information from either him or CJ. Do you think that's important?"

"We'll see." CJ appeared in the room with them, and she knew immediately that there was something different about her. Not magic—she would have a great deal of it now that she was mated—but there was something different about her that she couldn't put her finger on. "Come here, child. I have some questions that need to be put before you. I'm hoping with your help, we can narrow this down a little more."

"I hope I've not offended you, Melisandre. I meant no harm to you or yours but was only following the clues we had." She told the younger woman that she would have done the same if she had all the information leading to her as well. "Thank you for that."

After reminding CJ about the troll and what had happened, CJ stood and stretched out her wings. Melisandre was suddenly jealous of her. Whatever had happened to CJ in the last few days, it had made her far superior even to her. It was then that she saw her sigil. It moved all over her body. It wasn't until she turned back to them that she could pull her eyes away from the movement.

"It's like a filing cabinet for my past deeds. I only need to think of what I might have done, and my body finds it for me." She smiled at her, but again, it was the difference that startled her. CJ now had fangs. Long thin ones that Melisandre was sure she didn't get from her mate. "I'm evolving, I was told. Into what? No one seems to know. But I feel stronger daily. The troll. I went to see him and his mate's body. She was no more dead than I am. However, I said nothing to him at the time, and he seemed to think I wasn't believing him."

"He said she'd been killed by the pollution of his waterway." CJ said that was what she'd been told as well. "Then I don't understand. I believe you told me it had been taken care of. What happened?"

"He confessed to me—not that he wanted to— but he said he'd killed his own mate, and this was her sister. He liked her better anyway. Since I know for a fact that he broke about fifty laws, even for his kind, I put him in prison." Aurora asked if that had been the end of it. "I thought so at the time. The sister was also imprisoned, but since I could find no clues that told me she had anything to do with her sister's death, she was released a few days later. Could she be the one making all these threats to my family?"

"I'll figure this out." The troll was suddenly in the room they were in. The guards around her were holding onto chains made of the purest diamonds. The only way to hold a troll's magic was this way. Her mouth had been covered with a mask made of ground diamonds as well, so she couldn't cast a spell if she knew one. "Beatrice Troll, what do you have to say for yourself concerning the threats put on the life of Circe Jane Montgomery Steele?"

Melisandre nearly asked who Steele was when she realized it was the name Donald had adopted when he needed a last name. She didn't think she'd ever heard it before. The troll snarled at the three of them before she was allowed to speak.

"I know not a thing which you are talking about." Beatrice looked at her. "She should be in prison for all she's done to our family. Then this one," nodding at CJ, "this magical beast should be given to us so we might extract payment for how we've been treated."

"Payment for what? Don't lie to me." CJ's wings didn't just spread out behind her, but she moved in a way that lifted her off the floor, a foot or two about the head of the troll, which was quite a feat. The troll was twelve feet at least. "Tell me the truth, and I'll make your death quick."

"My death? You have no right to kill me. Not a smidgen of information that will lead back to me. You're the one that should be dead. Not my mate." CJ looked at Melisandre as she raised her hands above her head. Melisandre had the information before Beatrice spoke again. Standing, she told them what she knew.

"River was killed three days ago when Bea tried to get him out of prison. The wall that she'd been pushing against gave way under her weight, and it fell upon him. However, it should be noted that he was never her mate and that he wasn't the only one that killed Sal, Bea's sister. Bea led her to her death as surely as I'm standing here." CJ asked Bea if that was true. Since no one could lie to CJ, Bea gleefully said she'd helped River drown her. "She murdered two people. Plus, there was a babe that Sal was carrying when she met her death. Three deaths are now upon her shoulders."

"You can't count Sal's death against me. You have already declared that River did it." The laughter was much like nails down a chalkboard. CJ was the only one in the room that didn't seem bothered by it. "And since I'm stating now that River's death was wholly an accident, then you must believe me. I didn't love him, but he was good to me. Not like you are."

"Why did you have someone come to kill me last evening? Someone to break into my home and try to kill both myself and my mate while we were in bed? You should know that not only did this person confess he was being told to do this, but he also told me he'd rather die than have to go back to his boss and tell them he had failed. However, he didn't give me a name. Just that it was a female." That startled both Aurora and her when CJ spoke. Bea told her that she lied. "You know better than that. I cannot lie while in this room. Nor can you. Why did you send someone to kill us?"

"We were told if we were to kill the two of you that great riches would come our way. She told us that forever we'd be at her side. I deserve to be there when she rises up and takes over." CJ laughed and told her that was never going to happen. "She is closer than you think and will get you."

The snarl again was wet, and the splatter of it danced around the room until it hit the stone floor. Even as hard as it was, the acidy spit burnt deep holes into the stone and through it to the underground. If it had touched either of them or even something living, it would have eaten right through them until they were mutilated for life.

"The babe you carry will ruin it for all of us." That was it, Melisandre thought to herself. CJ was with child. Her eyes told all that knew her that CJ was carrying a life within her. CJ asked her why she thought that was going to happen. "Because these two will give you more than anyone deserves. You were not even raised as a faerie, and here you stand with so much power now that it blinds me. No, you need to be dead, so my kind can go about their fun without you causing us any trouble."

"You will wish for death." Bea looked at Melisandre, then at Aurora. She begged not just for her life but those of her children as well. "They're dead. I took care of them before coming here. Their short lives lay at your feet because you taught them your ways."

The bodies of four trolls, all of them considered adults by anyone who saw them, were lain on the floor between CJ and Bea by CJ's army. Bea's screams were cut off when CJ simply snapped her fingers. Not only did the sound stop, but Bea's mouth disappeared as well.

Melisandre could see that they'd not suffered at all but had been killed by a single stab to their heads. The spikes of iron were still within their skulls. She did wonder at the strength it would have taken to have put it through the skull of a troll. They had a skull thick enough, she knew, that very little could penetrate it—the reason they were so stupid. They had tiny brains in their head.

~*~

Don had never been asked to kill a troll before. If he was honest with himself, he'd thought they could only be killed by someone like Bancroft or the queens he was getting to know. He was being asked to do this because he was the second to Lord Bancroft. CJ had done her duty and found the guilty person. Now he was the one that would end her life after the trial.

Every time he said Lord Bancroft, even to himself, he had to stop himself from giggling. They were calling his childhood friend a lord. If only they knew him as he did. They'd rethink their position of calling him anything but a nutball.

The trial, or whatever this was, had been going on for several days now. He'd been told it would be short, and he'd finish her off for the crimes against her. But there had been so many other creatures to come forward to tell about the things that had been done to their kind by the troll that he was positive it was never going to end. Just today, there had been fifty-plus creatures that had said that Bea, her sons, or River had either killed a member of their family or had ruined their livelihood so that they were nearly dead themselves. Bancroft was in attendance as well, having only just found out that his own lands had been spoiled by the work of the trolls.

Did you know that when a troll is killed by a person such as myself, their history becomes written down and put in a library? I haven't any idea why. That's just what I was told. No one cares to find out why either. He asked CJ who read the accounting. *Good point. Other trolls. Do you think that's the reason for it? So they can see what other idiots did?*

I don't know why they'd have to go and read them in a book. Every troll in the land is here. What I find funny is that none of them seem to have any sympathy for any of the family of River and Bea. She told him that was sad and also expected. *Yes, I suppose so. I was wondering about your plans for after this trial. If it ever ends.*

I do have plans. The things I ordered are arriving daily. I've been putting this crap away since you left here.

By the way, you're going to be cutting down boxes when you return, not for the trash bin, but for the faeries. They've taken quite a shine to this stuff. The bubble wrap is the real hit. I think they're adding it to their playgrounds. He could see them jumping on it to hear it pop. Smiling to himself, he thought of what they might be doing with the cardboard. *Tonight we're going to figure out who the person is that is ordering the hits on me. I think I might have an idea, but right now, I'm trying hard to keep an open mind. Kelly and the other women are going to be helping me. Along with Bancroft's grannie. She's a hoot, by the way.*

He didn't have a clue, and that bothered him more than anything. Thinking about the death of Cody, he wondered if anyone would ever be able to look at CJ again without equating her with the way she'd killed the little creature. He would have thought it impossible to make such a small thing suffer the way he had, but then he'd never had to kill a troll before. Looking up when he heard the others shuffling around, he hoped it was the end. Not that he was looking forward to his part in this, but he wanted to just be home.

"We're breaking for lunch," Bancroft told him. That was another thing he didn't care for. They assumed that since he and some of the others were vampires, they needed to line up people for them. It was wrong in so many ways that he'd had to go away and have some time alone. "How about we go out in the gardens? I have a few things I'd like to discuss with you. It's not important, but it's just that I want your input on it."

"Sure." They were seated out in the most beautiful gardens he'd ever seen. The colors were bright and bold. The arrangement of the different plants seemed never-ending. It was difficult to tell where one plant ended and the other began. They blended so well as a whole. When Bancroft didn't start right away, Don told him what he'd been learning about since he'd gotten here. "Did you know there are at least a thousand faeries around you at any given time? I had no idea. Melisandre has been teaching me how to see them. I have magic for that, too, in the event you're wondering. It allows me to see them in a way that makes it easier for—"

"I have a plan." Nodding at Bancroft, he let him tell him rather than asking for details. Like what sort of plan did he have? Was it something to do with today? "Once, when I was a younger vampire, I purchased a great deal of land along the oceans. It wasn't all that expensive, but back then, no one was thinking they'd enjoy swimming in it. And those that did only went there when they needed a bath. Anyway, this plan I have is to sell it to put in hotels along the ocean for all of us to use. It would be a place where any of us could go and—"

"What are you talking about? I'm reasonably sure there are laws regarding that, but that's not the point. You're stalling. Tell me or not, but I'm here to listen if you want me to." He nodded and looked away before starting. "Bancroft, you're scaring me. What the hell is wrong?"

"I'm going to be a father." Don waited. He was as well, but they'd not shared that information with anyone as yet. "I don't have a lot of memories of my own parents. I'm terrified I'm going to fuck this up. What if one of my kids turns out to be like some of the ones we see here?"

"First of all, duh on you being a father. I think we all have noticed that Kelly is carrying around something. Secondly, you do know that you always fuck up your first one." Bancroft told him he wasn't helping. "Not my job, buddy, to make you feel good about being a parent. But the truth is, we're all terrified of that coming into our lives. And that's a good thing. I think people who don't think about being a good parent at least twenty times a day aren't going to be one. A good parent, I mean. Sheesh, Bancroft, I don't have any children, and every time I see one, I want to study it. I mean, like take it home and figure out how to take care of it. However, in all my trying to figure a kid out, I've noticed that they're all different. Even kids growing up in the same house could have a different personality for each one of them. That boggles the mind if you ask me."

"You aren't helping me the least bit now. What the hell do you mean, they could all be different? Do people raise their kids differently?" Don told him, of course, they did. "I could stake you right now. I'm not kidding one bit either. I could ram a stake through you and not think another thing about it."

"That's because we're all only children." Bancroft said that wasn't it at all. He wanted him dead because he was making the situation worse. "You love me, and we both know you're not going to kill me. Save that thought for when, if you have a daughter, she wants to date someone like you. Now that would give me nightmares."

"Shut the fuck up." Don was really enjoying this and thought that if Bancroft didn't kill him, he'd laugh himself into a stupor. "I don't even know why I thought you'd be at least sympathetic with me. Here I come to you with my woes, and you tell me shit that isn't the least bit helpful."

"Yes, it is, and you know it. I'm trying my best not to freak you out. No, that's not true. I am trying to do it a little and enjoying it too. But what you have to remember is that you aren't the only person to worry over this. Nor will you be the last. It is what it is, Bancroft. Why are you so twisted up about your child coming into the world?" He told him that they were having a daughter and a son. "Good for you.

You must be on top of the world. However, I surely do hope she takes after her mother. Both of them, actually. You are ugly. I'm sorry to have to tell you that, but it's the honest to god truth. You're an ugly man."

They were rolling around on the ground, sort of attempting to hurt one another, when Melisandre and Aurora came to where they were. Aurora fussed at them about her garden while Melisandre held onto the tree, laughing. Getting up from the ground, he offered his friend his hand.

"I'm not going to be any more sympathetic for you than you have been for me." Don told him he was glad to hear that. "You're really not afraid of being a parent? I find that hard to believe."

"I'm a very old and powerful vampire, the same as you. Anyone fucks with my kids and wife, I know it's been said thousands of times, but I do mean it when I say no one will ever find their bodies. However, I will take pictures and hang them around the house when someone calls on one of my daughters." Bancroft said he loved that idea. "You can use it if you wish. Even if I have to put the fear of me into their minds, my children will be as safe with dates as they would be with us, or I'll come down on them in such a way that their ancestors will be rolling in their graves."

"I'm not sure that talking to you had the desired effect I was hoping for, but it did calm me a little. Kelly is ready to toss me out of the house until the babies are entering college. Not that I think that will be calming enough for me, but she seems to think they'll be able to defend themselves by then." Bancroft stood up. "Thank you. You've made this old man feel at least marginally better."

"If you two are done with your patting each other on the back, do you think we could get this thing over with?" Melisandre was beginning to sound a great deal like CJ. Following them into the room, he was glad to see there weren't nearly as many people as there had been before lunch. "I've sent them all home. I don't think we need to hear any more about how the five of them had messed with their lives. Do you?"

"No. They weren't good people, so let's just get this over with." Melisandre nodded and started away, only to return to stand next to Don. "Something wrong?"

"Yes. So you know, I've had my people out searching for the person in charge of the things going on with CJ and you. I might have a name for you. But I don't want you to say anything to CJ." He said he could only do that until she asked him point-blank. "I know that, but this, if I'm wrong, will hurt our relationship, and I so enjoy having CJ around. She's been my rock since she was born, and I think I'd wither up and die without her around to talk to me." After asking her who it was she'd figured out, he sat down on the ground. "I know that it's a lot for you to take in, but I'm as sure about this as I am the friendship the two of us have."

"She'll have to be told, and soon. I don't think holding something this important from her is a good idea. Someone will need to inform her, and the sooner, the better." Melisandre nodded and sat down on the chair that suddenly appeared beneath her. "I'm assuming you wish for me to do it."

"I will. I just needed to see if you'd be there for me." Don thought about it and told her he'd tell her. "I don't want you to be the bearer of bad news, Don. I can tell her."

"I would rather if you don't mind." She told him whatever he thought was best. "Best? That would be to hunt this person down and give them the longest death I can make for them. However, I won't do that either. I'll go as soon as I have this taken care of."

"I have people watching both of them. I've been doing that all along, but this is so much more important than before." He had to agree with that. "All right. I'll wait here until you call to me. In the event that she has any questions or…I don't know, something else I can do for either of you."

He didn't know what that would be but decided he wasn't going to think about that. Today he had to kill a troll. Then later kill someone else. Things were not going to be happy around his home for some time, he worried.

As he entered the room, he was led to the open arena that surrounded the castle. He'd never known what the place was for until just this minute. The ground was made of sand and stone so that anyone bleeding here would not spoil the earth. As soon as Bea was bought out to him to kill, he waited for her sentencing to be read to her before he let go of his beast and did what few others could do. Kill a troll.

Chapter 7

CJ entered the back door of her sister's home just as she heard her calling for Cody. Not sure what she'd be wanting her faerie for, CJ pulled the shadows around her and slid deeper into the room until she could actually see Pfeiffer.

"Cody? Where are you? You were supposed to be here an hour ago." She stomped her foot, then yelled for him again. "Cody, if you don't come back here right this minute, I'm going to take away your sugar cubes for a month. Come on. I need you."

"Why?" Startling her sister, CJ sat down at the table and gave herself a tall glass of iced tea and several cookies. "I so love that I can eat whatever I want and not gain a single pound. I mean, it's not like I was carrying around a lot of weight in the first place, but knowing that makes this so much better. Why are you calling to my faerie, Pfeiffer?"

"We were to have a meeting. Here, let me get you something else. You shouldn't be eating sweets when it's so close to dinner." CJ pulled the cookies to her and told her to leave them alone. "That was harsh. What's up with you? Did someone say something to you?"

"No. Not yet. But you've not answered my question. Why are you calling for Cody?" She told her again that they had set up a meeting. "About what? I can't imagine what sort of meeting you'd be having with Cody. I mean, he only answers to me."

Pfeiffer sat down again and then got up to get herself a glass. While she was pouring tea, CJ tried to look into her mind. All she got for her efforts was a singsong about the alphabet. When Pfeiffer sat back down, she didn't reach for the cookies that were still on the plate. But she did crumble up a napkin. A sure sign that she was nervous.

"Just after you started going to school, even as young as you were, I was in awe of you. How you were so poised and seemed to be able to do just about anything. I know there were times when you'd get frustrated with me. Not having much in the way of confidence in myself the way you did. Then I met Robert. It seemed to me like things were going to go my way for a little while." Saying nothing, she watched the other woman. "Robert wasn't a nice person. Not even before we started dating. He wasn't abusive, not in the way that would show to anyone else, but you saw it, didn't you?"

"Yes. He would ride you until you didn't have anything left for anyone but him. Even when there were others around, your daughters, he seemed to think all that time you devoted to them wasn't right." Pfeiffer said that was how she felt as well. CJ wondered if she'd get to the point when she started speaking again. "Neither Sally nor Rachel are his. They're born of an affair I had with a kind man when I was younger. Robert knew. It was something he held over my head right up until he took his last breath."

"I don't know if you're aware of this or not, but you still haven't answered my question about Cody." She nodded, sipping her tea. Then she told her she was working up to it. "He's dead anyway. So is Benson."

"You killed them both." CJ told her she had. That she was going to kill the person that had hired them to kill her. "She's dead as well. That was why I was calling to Cody. To help me get rid of the body. Or, in this case, bodies."

She wasn't entirely sure what she was talking about, so let that hang there between them. Neither of them seemed inclined to speak right then, so she enjoyed her tea. Reaching out beyond where they sat, she could feel death, but not who it might have been.

Then it hit her.

"Rachel and Sally." Pfeiffer nodded, then started crying. "Why? I mean, why did they want me dead? Did they tell you?"

"Rachel has hated you since you were living with us. Sally? I don't know. I didn't know that at all, to be honest. They were always jealous of you that I am aware of, but enough to have you killed? It just didn't seem a possibility to me. Not my own daughters." Pfeiffer sobbed out how she'd found out. How she'd not known how far they had gone. "You see, they had to work so very hard for things. We never had a lot, and even though I was sure you had more than enough for all of us, I can understand why you didn't use it when we needed it. But they thought you should have paid for everything. Our home. Food. I'm not sure how they found out about it. Oh CJ, I'm so very sorry."

While offering her sister comfort, she thought about the girls, her nieces, while they'd been growing up. They would sometimes snap at her, make her a target of things, but they'd never indicated— She remembered a couple of times when she'd been out, and someone would hurt her. Lately, it had happened more and more, but she didn't think of her cousins as being part of it.

As she sat there thinking, more and more times when they had been nasty or hurtful to her came to light. The times she'd been caught out alone and been beaten badly were times when she was supposed to have met them someplace. Times they were getting together to have a little bit of fun. Thinking back on a lot of things, she could remember Cody being around them. He'd disappear for long periods of time that wouldn't be explained. He was with them, she thought now. No doubt about it now that she had time to put it all together in her mind.

"Did they tell you why?" Pfeiffer told her they'd not. "You killed your own children, Pfeiffer. They had to tell you something. How did you even figure it out?"

Getting up, she went to the trash can and pulled out several sheets of paper. It didn't look like anything until she looked at the ads Pfeiffer pointed to. As she read them, Pfeiffer explained how she'd figured it out.

"They put that in the paper looking for someone to come and kill you. Me too, Sally told me. There wasn't any point in having me around if I was just going to be nagging at them about your death. I was looking over the lonely hearts ads. Remember how we used to think how lonely you'd have to be to put an ad in the paper? At first, it only piqued my curiosity a little. But something in me made me keep going back to it. I'm ashamed to tell you that at first, I didn't get what they were asking. Then when I did, it was like being hit with a load of rocks." CJ was sure she might not have gotten it either at first. "Then I began looking at the wording of it. After that, the phone number. It's Sally's number. They used their own phone number to have someone call them who would kill off a relative for cash."

Honey, are you all right? She told Don she wasn't. And asked if he could bring not just the men with him but the women as well. *Have you killed her yet? I'm assuming you've found out your sister is the one that has been calling the hits on you.*

My sister? She glanced at Pfeiffer, then frowned. *She is telling me it was her daughters that hired the hitmen.*

It was her. Pfeiffer. I'm on my way. Don't let her hurt you. She stood up then, asking Pfeiffer if she wanted more to drink. *There is a pack of wolves outside the door to the kitchen. They've been watching over you since you arrived. Honey, Melisandre has been keeping an eye on her, and it's Pfeiffer, not the girls. Where are they? They need to be gotten out of the house as well.*

She said she killed them for me. And for the moment, I don't want to think about what she might have done to them. All right? Nervous and afraid for the first time in a long time, she took her time in filling their glasses with ice. Not that she had any plans of drinking anything from hers, but she did refill their glasses with the tea in the fridge. *I'm sitting at the kitchen table. When I got here, she was calling for Cody to help her get rid of the bodies. Oh, Don, I know she can't kill me, but please hurry.*

Sitting down, she smiled at Pfeiffer. It was all she could do not to get up and tear her throat out. She asked her about the bodies and what she had planned on telling the police. Pfeiffer, if she'd not been looking right at her, might well have gotten away with showing her madness. Even if it had only been a quick look for her.

"That was the reason I was trying to find Cody. He seemed to know a great deal about bodies and such." CJ frowned and asked her what she meant. "You know. Being magical like you are, I figured the two of you must have a great many bodies all over the place. For anyone that would try and take advantage of you."

Laughing a little, she told her she didn't know anyone that had taken advantage of her. "Certainly no one I've killed for it. I'm pretty easy about things. You know that." The anger again, also a little insanity. "What about you? Do you think I've taken advantage of you during our life together?"

The gun was pointed at her when Pfeiffer pulled it from someplace under the table. It didn't scare her as much as she thought it should have. CJ kept telling herself she was immortal. That no bullets or anything else would kill her. Painful, yes, she knew it would be that, but there would be no killing her. She was glad now she'd prepared herself for something like this by putting magic all around her unborn child.

"What are your plans with that, Pfeiffer? Do you think you can kill me? You can't, just so you know." The bullet entered her arm and threw her back, tipping over the chair. Standing up, fixing her chair, she sat back down and put her hand over the wound. "See, nothing will kill me."

"So you say." The next bullet hit her in the cheek. She might have been aiming for her head, but the natural reflex of moving out of the way had it entering her there. Don said they were there.

Wait. I have to see this through. He asked her if she was all right. *I am, actually. I think this is something she's been feeling for some time. But you will need to get the police here. She has killed her daughters.*

I know, honey. We'll take care of arrangements as soon as we get this part of it cleared up. She could agree with him on that note but watched Pfeiffer. *The police are here now. I guess the wolf pack could smell the blood and called them. They are parked around back, so be wary of leaving that way. I don't want you shot.*

I'm fine. I promise you. Pfeiffer screamed at her to die. "I'm sorry, I can't do that. I want you to know it makes me happy that I never got around to making sure you were immortal. I wish I had gotten to Rachel and Sally. It's a real shame you had to kill them off. I don't suppose you're like those talking killers, are you? Where you confess everything to the person you kill off right before the police arrive?"

"What is wrong with you? Can't you just die? Fucking bitch. You've always had everything, haven't you? All the money. The beautiful skin. No stretch marks would ever harm your body if you were ever to get knocked up. Little Miss CJ. Always the perfect person, even when I wanted you to be angry." CJ asked her why she'd be angry. "You never cared when I killed Robert. Do you have any idea how many times I left out the poison for you to see or find? What about being pissed that our parents are dead? You didn't shed a single tear for their demise either, did you? Miss Perfect."

"I did cry when your parents died. So you killed them as well. Why would you do that? What did they ever do to you?" Pfeiffer told her. "So bringing me into your family, that was the reason you hated them. I don't know if you realize this or not, but they didn't know I wasn't their child."

"Oh, but they did. I told them as I killed them. Made them realize what a burden they'd brought down on us. They certainly understood how upset I was at the end. I made sure of it." CJ could only stare at Pfeiffer. She'd been holding onto this grudge for that long? She asked her what her daughters had done to her. "Stretched out my body. But the thing that had me killing them both today was that they figured it out. Finally, someone could see my hard work. Now all I have to do is kill you, and things will be perfect for me."

"Doubtful you'd find anything to be perfect, Pfeiffer. You seem like a person who would never be satisfied even if you had everything you ever wanted. You'd be finding fault with it as well." Smiling at her, she felt like this was more than she thought would happen when coming here today. "You're the one that had it all as far as I can remember. You had your parents. Your husband, though he wasn't much of a person. At least you led me to believe that. Now that I'm thinking, you never did allow me to see him for what he really was, did you? Then there are your daughters. They loved you, you know. I guess your little maneuvers were more than they thought their dear mother was capable of."

"You should have seen their faces. When I hit Rachel in the head with the axe, I was sure Sally was going to jump me. But all she did was stare at her sister until she was joining her on the floor. Knocking her in the head seemed anticlimactic after all my planning to get here. But they were both out of my hair. I might well have gone a little overboard in killing them, but there wasn't going to be any getting back up again for them. It was a wonderful feeling being able to take all my frustrations out on them. Now it's your turn." CJ asked her about Rachel being hurt in the car accident.

"Well, of course, I did that too. It worked just the way I wanted it to. Brought you to me so I could finish this once and for all."

Come in if the police are satisfied with it all. I'm sick with all this.

Don entered right behind the police. CJ held Pfeiffer in a holding pattern with her magic so no one else would be hurt. The police then went to the upper floors to check on the bodies of the other two while Don took her outside into the fresh air. Making sure that her wounds were healed, CJ let Don hold her. It was the best medicine in the world if you asked her.

~*~

Melisandre thought this was one of the best ideas she'd ever had. Once this thing with Pfeiffer was finished, she could move on with her life. Get things in order and try and figure out the meaning of her life.

Everyone had their own idea as to what their meaning to life was. She'd known that all her life but had somehow forgotten about it. Now that she'd been given a new start, a new beginning, Melisandre was going to make sure she lived every day like it was her last. Make every second count and have fun while on her way.

"You wanted to see me?" Smiling at CJ, she asked her to have a seat. "This is nice. I didn't know you owned a home on this side. I love the bright and bold colors. You should have been an interior designer or something."

"I'll have to add that to my list of things to try. I'm retiring. Well, not retiring, but leaving my position as queen of faeries for good." She loved that she could shock CJ. Especially when she knew CJ had seen so much more than she had in life. "I've spoken to Aurora, and she said she would support me in what I wanted. You know how hard I took the fact that Cody, someone you thought you could trust, had been out to have you murdered. It bothers me on so many levels how I was so blind to it."

"It's not like I did any better with noticing things. I sometimes find myself thinking of how we grew up. The little things I'm only just now seeing the way I should have right away. It's hurtful to think that me being hidden away by going to her parents was such a problem for Pfeiffer that she had to kill her entire family over it." Melisandre knew she'd taken the deaths of her nieces hard. She might well have too, she thought. "Don and I are going to go on a honeymoon soon. There are so many places I've never seen. We're also going to have a baby."

"I knew of the child. I cannot be happier for you." She needed to get to the point, and soon. Aurora was coming soon to talk to her about things as well. "I've asked that you take over my job."

Smiling at her, she knew immediately that CJ didn't understand. "What job? I mean, I know you want to step down from doing your work, but surely you don't mean—" Her face told it all. "Oh no, you didn't. You did not put me in for your job as queen of the faeries. I refuse it. That's what I'll do. Refuse it."

"I don't think you can now." She asked her why not, and Melisandre put out her hand. "This has been made for you. The faeries think it's great that they are not only going to have you as queen, but they got to make your crown."

"No." When CJ stood up, she watched her pace. She also began talking to herself, in faerie. When she suddenly stopped and turned to her, Melisandre couldn't help it. She began to laugh. Hard. "I was speaking something else, wasn't I?"

"Faerie. You've picked it up a good deal faster than I did." There was no stopping her laughter now. Melisandre laughed until tears streamed down her face and collected on her bosom. "If you could see your face right now, I think you'd laugh as well."

"No I would not. Also, you need to stop right now before I hurt you." Melisandre pointed out that she couldn't hurt her. Not ever. "Then, by all means, laugh it up. Make fun of the person that has not only been bamboozled into something she never wanted but has no way of retaliating."

"Oh, you know you love me, CJ. You also know there isn't a better person for the job than you." Tea and other delights appeared on the table in front of her. Her appetite had returned now that she'd been able to talk to CJ, and she was most assuredly hungry. "You would have figured out about the other faeries long before I did. I don't know how anyone missed Cody being turned around, but Benson would have been found out by you had you spent any time with him. I've been very lax on my duties as queen, at least in reference to the people who work for me. That's why I'm going to be staying on as your helpmate in the area of the flowers. That part I know, and well. You will be the one that keeps an eye on the faeries and others. I didn't do that."

"I'd like to say I noticed it too, but I didn't. Cody had only been with me for about the last ten years, I think. So from what I've been able to find out, he was working with Pfeiffer since before that." She took the little cup of tea and changed it into a large glass of ruby red juice. Smiling as she sipped her tea, she wondered if CJ had even noticed that she was wearing the crown yet. "I'm very leery of trusting the faeries right now. I know it was only the one, but he did such a good job of hiding in plain sight that I don't know what to do about trusting anyone to be that close to me again."

"I don't blame you. Not at all. However, with the magic that you get by being queen, Aurora has enhanced your ability to see lies when they're put before you." She set down her cup and regarded the younger woman. "I'm sorry about all this, CJ. You do know I've always loved you. However, I think you being queen will do so much more for them than I was ever able to do. No, that's not right. I was able to do it, but I was too focused on a single thing. That's why, as you can multitask better than anyone I've ever met, nothing like this will get by you for too long before you're able to fix it. You'll also be fair about your punishments. Although I have to tell you, I've never seen the workers working so hard before. I do believe they're afraid of you. Which isn't a bad thing. That's another thing I did. I was much too friendly with all of them. I made a great many mistakes."

"We all made mistakes. Not just on Cody, but a great many things." She looked so sad that Melisandre wanted to give her comfort. "The council is taking care of Pfeiffer. She'll stand trial in front of the Magical Creatures Board. I wasn't sure how that was a case they'd take, but since she took Cody from his duties for him to work for her, that is their territory. Also, because she was willing to kill me and others of this world. If there is anything left of her when she's finished with them, they'll allow her to be put before a human court. But from what I've been told, she won't be long for this world."

"No, she won't." Aurora appeared in the room, and like she did whenever she was before the queen, Melisandre bowed low. CJ just sat on the couch and drank her drink. While she knew that CJ respected the queen, she wasn't any too happy with being picked to take over the job that Melisandre was leaving open.

"You're supposed to pay me homage, CJ." The younger woman snorted. "Yes, that is what I thought you'd do. However, I have it on good authority that you're going to make a great queen. You'll do this world a—"

"I didn't say I'd take it." Aurora sat down and poured herself some tea. "Did you hear me? I'm not taking the job. I'm newly married. I have a baby on the way, and I don't have time to take anything else on my plate at the moment."

"You're wearing the crown." Aurora sipped her tea as CJ cursed, trying to remove the crown that marked her as the queen of faeries. "It wouldn't have stayed there if you didn't want the job. Nor if you weren't going to be good at it. I put that in the spell when I approved it from the faeries. Whatever other things you have going on at the moment will not be nearly as difficult for you if you'd allow someone to help you. I don't mean any of us, but Don. Did you know he's very worried about you? That he's not sure what to do for you?"

"I told him every time he asked—about a million times a day—that I'm fine." Aurora said she wasn't. "I am too. I would think that someone as old as rocks and dirt would know to keep out of other people's business. Christ, don't you have anything else to do but nib at me?"

"No, not at the moment. I will tell you this if you care to listen. You're not going to enjoy anything as much as you do being queen, CJ. It will afford you so much power that you'll never want for another thing." She told her she wanted them both to leave her the fuck alone. "No you don't. You're hurting. I can see it. You feel betrayed, which I would be feeling as well. But most importantly, you feel as if you've let down your cousins. You didn't, child. Their mother did."

"She killed them both." Aurora asked if she knew why Pfeiffer had murdered them. "I don't know. I wish…every hour of every day I wish I'd given them the immortality. Rachel and Sally would still be alive had I only gotten around to helping them."

"CJ, do you know that when a person is hurt badly—a broken neck, broken skull—that cannot be helped with immortality? A person will live forever but will have those things still with them. Rachel's head had been bashed in. Pfeiffer had taken an axe to her head. She would have been mentally incapacitated even had she been immortal. I could have taken that from her, but she would have suffered needlessly in the meantime. Sally was much worse. Not only had her head been bashed in, but her spine had been severed. She would not have been able to feed herself.

Been able to go to the bathroom. Not anything after her mother had hurt her."

"I wasn't allowed to see their bodies. The coroner told me it would be better if I only kept the memories of them when they were alive." Aurora told her that he was good for telling her that. "It still seems so surreal to know that Pfeiffer had held this grudge against me for so long. Even before I was old enough to figure out I wasn't really her sister. Now she's going to be gone from my life, along with her daughters, and I have no family left."

"That's not true. You have us. All the faeries. As well as Don and the rest of the kiss. Soon you're going to have a child that will love you as much as we do. You've gained more than you've lost. I know it's a terrible loss. I, too, have lost like this before, but you're a strong person and will come out all the better for it. At least—and I want you to think about this—at least you've been able to find a love who has and will love you unconditionally." She asked Aurora if she meant Don. "He would be included, but I was talking about myself. And I'm sure Melisandre. We both have taken you to our hearts and will never not be there for you. Also, I know you say you don't want to be the queen of the faeries, but you really should think of all the good you could do. That I know you will do. You have a brilliant mind, CJ. You also make sure the earth is much better than when you left it."

"You and I will work well together as well. As I said before, I'll take the planting seasons part of the job, and you won't have to worry about that at all. That will leave you all the time you need or want on making sure that all the faeries have what they need. I know Lord Bancroft has set aside a great many acres of land for us to use." CJ said she knew that. "You will also have the army at your beck and call. More than you do now. All of them will work with you, not just the army you have had. It's my understanding that Lord Bancroft has given you full authority to take out the bad vampires when you find them. That is such a wonderful thing, my child. To be able to make sure they aren't hurting the land with their death and mayhem."

"I need to think about it. And to talk it over with Don." She eyed her hard. "You've already talked to him, haven't you? You certainly had all your ducks lined up to shoot the shit out of them, haven't you? Damn it, I don't want to do this."

After she left them there to go and speak to Don, Melisandre and Aurora continued to talk as if CJ had already taken the job. It occurred to her that at some point, they were going to have to talk to her about her pay, as well as what was in store for the couple when they did start working with the faeries.

"I have already set into motion that her house is readied for them. Also, after speaking to Don,

I believe they're going to put in a place just for the faeries to live in during the colder months. I believe that alone will keep them very happy." Melisandre asked if she thought she'd turn them down. "No. She wants it, but as she was telling you before I arrived, she isn't very trusting right now. I hurt for her with that feeling. Once she is working, I think it will be easier for her to move on. The deaths of so many are what is weighing her down. Her guilt, too, for not seeing things earlier."

"She also told me she believes Cody had been working with Pfeiffer for a while before Cody came to be her faerie. That is why she wasn't able to see what had changed about him. What have you done with Cody's family? I think he had himself a mate at one time. But I do believe she's gone." Aurora told her what had happened to the mate but that he'd had a girlfriend of sorts. "I'm so sorry for that. I didn't know his mate, but to have been killed by a car is a nasty way to go. I think that will be another thing CJ will be able to teach the little ones. How to avoid being hit by a car. So many are lost that way."

"I agree. Bancroft is not only setting aside the land for us to use, but he has also gifted the faeries all manner of things they may have. Cardboard being one of the many things they can upcycle. CJ is also taking some of the crafts they make and selling them. The coin they get, it goes to getting specialty items they cannot make. Small cut glass for windows. Also, she is looking for a potter that will make things such as garden bowls for them. I have to admit, I never thought of a small bowl that they could use to put their gardens in. They like to move them around to get the best light in the day." She said she'd only just heard about it. "There are also things I have never thought of to help with costs. You know as well as I do that they use whatever they can to work with, but some of the gems they find, they're being made into jewelry to sell. The money will be used for helping families that might have lost someone or when they are being relocated. I wouldn't have thought that would have been an expense, but CJ not only found out but has made a way for them to have a home when they get to their new area. Do you know how much she's done without even taking the position she doesn't know if she wants?"

"Much more than I did." Aurora told her that's not what she meant. "No. I know that. I do. But I did nothing to help them. Only kept them working on flowers and seeds. I know that is an important part of our job, but I forgot to look at the entire picture about what they were giving up or going without to work so hard. I know now that I have to be a task maker, but also I need to pay more attention. I believe CJ will help me with that as well."

They continued to speak for over an hour about

what a wonderful job CJ would be doing. Even going over some of the things that Melisandre had been able to take care of. Aurora was a good queen. She was there for a person when they needed it, but she never pulled back when there was something that needed to be said. She liked that most about her.

Also, Aurora was quick to compliment you in front of your peers or workers. But when you needed to be spoken to about something that was wrong, she never did it where others could hear. Not that Aurora had to speak to her behind closed doors often, but when she did, no one was any the wiser about it.

"I must be getting back. I have some paperwork I need to go over before I can speak to them when they return. Don is giving her his support, as I knew he would, but he is leaving the answer up to her. He is a good man." Melisandre agreed. "Will you contact me if you need anything? Oh, before I forget—too much going on again—you will live here if you wish or in the other realm. It is up to you. It's doubtful to me that CJ will want to be here anymore than she needs to be. She so enjoys the things the other world can offer her."

"I would love to live here if you don't mind." Aurora told her it was up to her. Melisandre thanked her. "It's home for me now. I think I would be lost in the other world."

"As would I."

After Aurora left, Melisandre settled into her work. The charts she had for planting were all hers, something she'd worked very hard on. Now that she could devote all her time to planting, Melisandre couldn't be happier.

Chapter 8

Gracie watched the water flow over the dam. She'd been coming here to this spot for years now, and it was always different. Today there were families having a nice day in the warm sunshine with a picnic basket and all. There were dogs, too, playing with their masters and retrieving whatever it was they tossed for them to return. Small and big kids were chasing each other, some of them racing the clouds as well. When someone sat down beside her, she didn't bother looking. She had an idea she knew just who it was.

"Why anyone would want to eat out of doors is beyond me. Bugs and grass all over a person. And the food is forever cold. Even things that should not be. Who would have believed that humans would eat a cold chicken leg?" She smiled at Craig. "What have you been doing since we spoke last? Have you gotten things on your end under control yet?"

"I have. There are two shipments going out in the morning. Hopefully, they'll end up where they're supposed to be. Yesterday there was a big brew-ha-ha over some damaged merchandise that was sent to them by mistake, but they got it taken care of quickly." He asked her about the trip that was being planned for next week. "I still can't find anyone that is going. There is a flight plan made out for the company jet, but no names on the schedule. I'll keep working on that. I have about four days left to find the manifest of who is going."

"The boss would like you to pull yourself from the job site a few days earlier than we planned. He thinks that once things start falling apart around them, they'll start looking harder at the people who were only just hired. You've been there how long now?" She told him. "Yes, well, I'll see what he wants you to do. Getting fired might be hard for you. I'm hearing about how much you've contributed to the work there."

"It's all right. Whatever is needed." She looked out beyond where they were sitting at the families again. "Do you suppose there is a person out there for us, Craig? I don't mean a family, but someone we can have some fun with and perhaps share a good bottle of wine with?"

"It's doubtful to me that anyone would want an old queer vampire to share anything with them." She laughed but kept watching the families. "Why are you asking? I've never heard you wish for bedpartners or even someone to share a meal with before. Are you getting too old for this, my dear?"

"No. Goodness, no. And before you ask, no, I'm not bored either. I'm just being silly, I guess." She saw that someone was setting up a few tables. Perhaps a party was going to be going on. Gracie loved birthday parties for the little ones. As she watched the people putting tablecloths on the long tables, she spoke to Craig without turning. "When I was a child, there was a kid in my class that was having a party. Everyone was invited, even me this time. But once at the house, I knew I'd only been invited because his mother had insisted everyone be there. The gift I had was cheap and not wrapped as well as the other things. I never went to another one after that. Have you ever been to a child's party, Craig?"

A playpen was set up for a baby, and Gracie wished she was close enough to see the child. She'd bet it had pudgy little legs and fat cheeks. The cutest babies always seemed to be ready to explode with good humor and chubby legs. Turning to ask Craig if he heard her, she saw that he was gone.

"Not nice, Craig."

Before she turned back to the scene below her, she saw that there was ash on her clothing. A great deal of it. Counting to fifty slowly so she could think, she knew it was important to get her ass in gear and out of there. Still seated, she took the briefcase Craig carried with him everywhere he went and shoved it up under her shirt. Then she pulled out her weapon, checking to make sure it was loaded and ready to go. Reaching down to pretend to tie her shoes, she pulled out one of the extra clips and put it in her front pocket. Stretching and looking around, she stood up and made her way out of the area as quickly as she could without drawing attention to herself.

It took her four hours to lose the tag she had on her. Then another hour for her to find the man and kill him. Before she could pull the trigger on her weapon to take him out, he shot her once in the shoulder. Christ, it had knocked her back on her ass, but she'd been able to get up and get rid of the bloodstain before anyone could get to it. Chemicals were forever on her for that very move.

Whoever he was working with, they'd prepared their shooter well. He didn't have prints on his hands or anything that would tell him apart from every other male in the world. She did, however, take a bit of his blood in a vial and put it in her case.

Knowing that going home would be a terrible move, she made her way to the safehouse she had set up. There she'd be able to get money, a list of contacts, as well as more weapons. Gracie would also be able to fix her wound and get a grip on herself. It wasn't that she would freak out, but she needed to know who would kill an operative while sitting right next to another one.

After pulling the bullet free of her shoulder and cleaning up the wound, she took a large bottle of whisky off the shelf and drank straight from the bottle. Sitting down in the kitchen, she opened Craig's briefcase and was startled to see her name on an envelope.

Getting herself a glass, knowing that Craig would be looking down on her, upset that she was drinking from the bottle, she poured the liquid to the top and sat back down. Emptying out the rest of the things in the case, she set the letter aside.

Her employment file was in his case, along with his own. She set those aside, wondering why he'd have them on his person. Then she looked at the map he had, as well as a few notes that had been written on it. Craig would never stoop to using GPS. He told her it was too easy to trace. She didn't use it either. Nor even a cell phone.

Putting the things in piles, Gracie put her hands over the case to see if he had hidden anything else in the thing that no one would be able to find without her kind of magic. Finding the small piece of silver there, she knew without looking at the note with it that it was what had killed his lover. Contrary to what he said to people, Craig was a heterosexual and had had a very long and wonderful life with his wife Margaret before her death, before Gracie had even been born.

Pulling the envelope to her, she opened it up carefully and laid not only the money to the side but what looked like a passport. Opening the letter, she read what her only friend in the world had left her.

"If you're reading this, I'm dead. If I am, I hope you have the good sense not to call it to the office nor to let anyone else know. I'm dead—having others know will not bring me back no matter how much you'll miss me." She would too. More than she would anyone. Taking another drink from her glass, she refilled it as she continued. "You've more than likely gone over everything I have in this case before reading this letter. Good girl. I've taught you well. However, don't let that go to your head. There are things afoot that you must now be made aware of. Like there is someone in the office looking for you. Through me. I do believe he will likely kill me to get to you. Don't go looking for him. If you do, you might as well sign your own death warrant. You'll need to get yourself someplace safe for now."

She had to pause in her reading. Gracie knew he'd make sure she was safe, even after death. The man had a way about him that would make her pissed off at him one minute, then wondering how she'd ever lived without him. The living without him was hitting her very hard right now.

"There is a man that I neither know nor have spoken to other than through our link. He is the king of all our kind. You must go to him. Don't even think about telling me no. You will do it because I'm dead, if for no other reason than that. I cannot go to the afterlife wondering if you're safe too." Nodding to the letter, she said to him that she'd go. "Good for you, my dear child. His name is Bancroft Dalton. He is, by all accounts, a good man, as well as a man that gets things done. You will go to him, and he will not only keep you safe, but he will make sure justice will be served for my death."

After reading the rest of his missive to her, she found out that she was his only heir. Not that she really was, but he told her she was his child, no matter that he didn't sire her. After gathering up the other things he'd sent with her, she found the key he'd mentioned too. She'd be able to get in and out of the bank holding whatever he wanted her to have without anyone being the wiser.

Gracie made plans to leave this place first thing in the morning. There was nothing here to indicate she'd been here at any time, but she would still destroy the place after she left. Not a soul lived in the building but her, and even though she owned it, no one would ever be able to track down the rightful owner. She had learned a great deal from her friend, the vampire.

Gracie took a long hot shower and figured out her plans for the next morning. Gathering up all the things she would need—guns, ammo, as well as her first aid kit—she put it all in her magical backpack. It would hold a car, and she'd be able to carry it if it came down to that. Studying the passport and gathering the money up with what Craig had given her, she ate a bowl of cereal that had expired three years ago dry and set up her bed. Tomorrow she'd be leaving this country forever. There wasn't any reason for her to return now that her friend was gone.

By six the next morning, she was inside the vaults at the bank. The key she had opened one box that led her to three more. Taking all the money and gems out of them, she put them in the bag. Also, she was able to find Craig's will, along with the deeds to all his properties. Not bothering to read them right now, she slipped out of the vault, then the bank, before anyone came into work.

The second place she went to was an unmarked grave. There were no dates on it. Nothing to indicate that someone was buried beneath the large headstone. She took out the bullet that had been left on the seat where Craig had been sitting and shoved it into the ground along with the little piece of silver. Putting her hand on top of the ivory stone, she felt the marker give under her fingers and pulled the last thing she needed with her. A thumb drive.

It was updated daily and brought here under cover of darkness and vampire skills. She didn't know what was on it but had been told no less than fifty times a day that she was to get it and take it with her if she needed to run. Today was the first time she'd been able to open the mechanism. More than likely because the magic knew Craig was gone.

There were two cars for her to use. Gracie took the one that had fewer people lingering outside the building. She didn't recognize anyone as being operatives, but it made her no less careful of getting in and out. By the time she was pulling into the airport to get a flight out of the country, not only was the building she'd been in last night nothing but rubble but Craig's place as well as his desk at work were destroyed. She never worked there often enough to have a desk, and Craig had already taken her file.

The flight took off on time, and she settled down to sleep. Or at least pretended to do so. She was wearing enough of a disguise that no one would recognize her. And since she'd been getting magic from Craig, no one would be able to describe her the same way as the other patrons on the plane. She was a ghost. What most of the people called her where she had worked.

By the time the latest plane she was on landed

at the airport in Columbus, Ohio, she'd been around the world three times. Getting off the plane at each stop made it easier for her to see if she was being followed. However, her shoulder was aching badly by then, and she was exhausted.

Without any kind of driver's license or even a photo identification, she wasn't able to rent herself a car. But that was easy enough to work around. Stealing one of the cars from the lot, she was well on her way to the king's house four days after Craig was murdered. The car, like the other things she'd used, would be destroyed when she got to the king. He'd better not be some blowhard, or she'd have to figure out a way to kick his ass. Settling into one of the empty buildings on the outskirts of town, she was ready for some sleep. Pulling out a sleeping bag as well as some clean clothing, Gracie closed her eyes and fell into a fitful sleep.

Gracie would do as the king wanted, but only so far. She wanted to take some of the money she'd saved up and buy an island. Someplace accessible either by flying in or taking a ship. After her years of service to her government, Gracie felt as if she deserved something nice. To not give a shit about anything else was her plan.

~*~

Bancroft hung up the phone. Craig Anderson had been killed five days ago. Not only had he been killed, but someone had gotten into his bank and taken everything he'd had stored in there. Bancroft hoped it was his friend, Gracie James, and not some random ass that had just happened to know where to look. When Kelly joined him in the office, she sat on his lap and asked him if he was all right. "I am. We're to have a visitor in the next few days. I don't know anything about her other than her name. Grace James. I'm not entirely sure that is her real name either. She was a friend of someone that contacted me a month ago when he was having trouble at his work."

"The Anderson man." He nodded. "You said he worked for the IBC. I don't remember what you told me that meant."

"Identity-based cryptography. I'm not sure in what capacity he worked for them, but I know it was very hush-hush. The woman, as I said, I don't know anything about. But she meant a great deal to the man, and he wanted me to protect her at all costs." Kelly asked him if she worked there as well. "I don't know. She might well have. When he called me, he told me there were some very unsavory people looking to get to Gracie—that's what he called her. And if they got her, they'd not kill her but use her. Again, I haven't any idea what that might mean."

"More than likely, she's magical. But not a vampire." Bancroft told her he didn't believe she was. "I guess we'll find out when she arrives. Do you know when?"

"That was her on the phone. She called to tell me she'd be at the restaurant in town at six tonight and that she'd see us there. I don't think she's all that trusting. If I were to bring anyone with me other than you, I can kiss her ass goodbye. I'm not sure what that means either, other than literally kissing it goodbye, but she said I was to go only with you." Kelly asked him if he would. "Yes. I'm not sure why, but I feel like I can trust her to do what she says. The girl knows she can't kill me, but she can put me in a world of hurt. I believe her. Also, and this is from Craig, Gracie is a good deal stronger than she looks, and I'm not to let her wallow in her own pain of losing him if I can help it. They were very close."

"All right. Do you think she'll stay here?" Bancroft shrugged. "Does she need medical attention? Clothing? Money, or even a nice warm meal?"

After each question, he shrugged. When she smacked him on the chest, he told her once again that he knew nothing about her. The one and only thing he did know about her was that she needed to be protected. That it was for all mankind. However, he didn't tell Kelly that. That would be just like telling her to go see the woman and get answers.

By the time they were ready to go, he was no closer to getting information than he had been before. He'd not done any kind of search on either Craig or Gracie. But he did hear about the explosion of a building, as well as a stolen car at the local airport. Nothing more than that was out there, but he had a feeling it was Gracie.

At five-thirty, they were seated in the only sit-down restaurant in town. He noticed that Clyde and Brian were there as well but didn't invite them to join them. Bancroft hoped that Gracie didn't think they'd been asked to come here on his behalf. Talking to this woman was his top priority.

He ordered a glass of wine from the waitress that came by, and Kelly asked for some juice. Looking around the place, he wondered why they'd not eaten here before. Taking a small sip of the wine, he noticed a small piece of paper was sticking out of the butter. He might not have noticed it at all, but when Kelly had cut into it, it stuck out.

Pulling the note out, he read it. What surprised him the most was that it was written in the old language of the vampire. The second thing was that his waitress was Gracie. She came back with a second basket of bread when he was trying to decide what to do now.

"The room is on pause." He looked around and was dismayed to see that Kelly was not moving either. "I don't know her. I don't know your ass either, but I was told you were a good man. I have to have a doctor see me as soon as possible. Only someone you trust. I was shot the day Craig was killed, and it's not healing well."

"Can you heal yourself?" She told him she couldn't but could heal others. Even so far as to bring them back from death. "I see. Actually, I don't know what to think about that. Where are you staying?" When she didn't answer him, Bancroft put out his hand. "You don't trust well, I was told. I will give you a sip of my blood so you can speak to me at any time."

I don't need it. I don't even need to touch you to be able to speak to you like this. His heart started racing when she did speak to him. "I'm not sure what else I might have gotten from Craig's death, but enough to get me in and out of situations that aren't of my making. I was human when I met him. A child. He took me in, trained me, and kept me out of trouble. I owe him my life, and anything else he might have wanted from me. But he asked for nothing. I was told you could protect me."

"I can. I will." She nodded and stood up. "What happens now? Those others over there. I didn't know they would be here."

She just smiled at him as the room began moving again. Gracie asked him if he was ready to order.

After placing an order, he told Kelly what had happened. Just as he'd thought she would, she was pissy. Then she thought it was funny. He'd been outmagicked by a young woman. When their dinner was brought to them, not only was the meal perfect, but their waitress was different. He supposed she'd gotten what she wanted from him and would get back with him later.

The man Brian is in trouble with his family. Nothing new, it sounds like, with the people you hang around with. He will need you to help him with money very soon, or he'll go to prison. Not a good place for a vampire, I'm guessing. He told her it wasn't. *The other man, Clyde, he's having a wonderful time staying at your home. However, he's bored out of his mind and wishes you'd give him something to do. He needs neither money nor anything else. He's just a man used to having plenty to do all the time. The others in your household seem to be doing well.*

Are you going to go to my home? I'm assuming you know where it is by now. She told him she did but wasn't going there just yet. She had two things to fix yet. *Something I should be aware of?*

No. But the new queen of faeries needs someone to slap her around. She's in over her head and is going to fail, she thinks. I don't know how she thinks she will since she's been taking care of the little people for some time now. Just hit her upside the head, and she'll be fine. He said she'd hurt him if he did that. *Yes, I suppose she would. I was going to ask if you'd do that when I was around, but that might distract me too much from my job. Also, the man Ramon, he's a physician. I'll need him to look over my wound as soon as tomorrow. I'll meet him at your home.*

There was no more communication from her for the rest of the night. He did have a splendid meal with Kelly, and the food was fantastic. His bill, he was told, was paid already, and he only needed to leave a tip. The note with his paid bill said he was to leave a good one or someone would take him to task. Bancroft was still laughing as they headed home.

While he didn't know anything about Gracie, nor what sort of trouble she might be in, he was looking forward to tangling with her. He had a feeling she was a hellcat like the women in the family. Kelly, too was happy to know she could hold her own with him. He was just too pleased to get upset about anything right now.

Before You Go...

HELP AN AUTHOR

write a review

THANK YOU!

Share your voice and help guide other readers to these wonderful books. Even if it's only a line or two, your reviews help readers discover the author's books so they can continue creating stories that you'll love. Log in to your favorite retailer and leave a review. Thank you.

Kathi Barton, a winner of the Pinnacle Book Achievement award as well as a best-selling author on Amazon and All Romance books, lives in Nashport, Ohio, with her husband, Paul. When not creating new worlds and romance, Kathi and her husband enjoy camping and going to auctions. She can also be seen at county fairs with her husband, who is an artist and potter.

Her muse, a cross between Jimmy Stewart and Hugh Jackman, brings her stories to life for her readers in a way that has them coming back time and again for more. Her favorite genre is paranormal romance, with a great deal of spice. You can visit Kathi on line and drop her an email if you'd like. She loves hearing from her fans. aaronskiss@gmail.com.

Follow Kathi on her blog: http://kathisbartonauthor.blogspot.com/